As the youngest spiritual advisor of Foshana in over a century, Sai-Jun performs his duties with a single-mindedness that comes from years of study and training . . . or at least, he'd like to, except that a fateful encounter with a certain young man nearly a year ago continues to invade his thoughts. Worse still, that young man is Shen-Fei, son of General Shen-Ya, whose dangerous temper has inspired Sai-Jun's intense dislike.

For all his father's ambitions, Shen-Fei has no wish to follow in his footsteps as a warrior. Instead, his passion is for drawing — something the general will not tolerate. He also hides a dark secret that he dares not share with anybody — not even the one person who might be able to help.

With emotions threatening to come to a head amid the ever-present game of politics, will secrets be exposed too late? And even once they're revealed, will Sai-Jun and Shen-Fei be able to resolve past misunderstandings and rekindle their lost love?

Marked by the Gods
Copyright © 2022 Diana Waters
ISBN: 978-1-4874-3494-6
Cover art by Martine Jardin

Published by eXtasy Books Inc

Look for us online at:
www.eXtasybooks.com

Marked by the Gods

By

Diana Waters

PROLOGUE

Thunder boomed overhead. In the dimness of the palace library, blessedly abandoned at this hour, a few guttering lamps fixed to the wall threw shadows over Sai-Jun's face as Shen-Fei drew him closer.

They kissed—Shen-Fei didn't know who did so more fiercely, but by the time they parted briefly to draw breath, his own lips felt bruised and swollen. Sai-Jun growled something—Shen-Fei didn't know what, the words lost to the pounding of the rain—and he didn't much care. Together, they dragged each other across the room until Shen-Fei's body met bare stone wall, deliciously cool against overheated skin.

He felt drunk, though he'd had little more than a cup of sweet red wine. If anything, Sai-Jun was probably the drunker of the two. Though usually outwardly self-possessed to the point of coldness, tonight, in response to the many toasts celebrating his official appointment as spiritual advisor—the youngest person to be afforded the role in over a century—Sai-Jun had been given no other option but to politely accept. His normally pale features were faintly pinkened, his somber elegance thrown slightly off. Or maybe more than slightly, Shen-Fei supposed, half-gasping, almost tempted to laugh at the thought, as he was turned and shoved unceremoniously against the wall once more when he attempted to kiss Sai-Jun again. Not that he minded. Gods above, why had it even taken this long? He'd been interested in Sai-Jun for years, had thought Sai-Jun had been interested too . . .

"Ahhh . . ." He smothered another gasp, this one turning into a groan as he felt Sai-Jun's hands over him, probably as inexperienced as Shen-Fei's own, but intent in their fevered wanderings. But when he felt Sai-Jun begin to tug insistently at his robes, he suddenly remembered, and the sweat over his body turned cold. "No. Don't. Here, just . . ."

He fumbled at the bottom of his robes instead, pulling them up, a little ashamed of this wanton display, but there was no helping it. It was this or nothing—and he badly wanted *this*, enough to risk everything. Enough to risk being discovered, in spite of what was at stake. If he could just have this without Sai-Jun seeing too much . . .

His heart, beating frantically, felt as though it might burst from his chest. Just as long as Sai-Jun didn't know. And he wouldn't. Shen-Fei wouldn't allow it. His secret would remain safe, so long as Sai-Jun took the gods-be-damned hint and just—

"Oooh . . ." Shen-Fei shuddered as he felt the surprisingly careful intrusion, fingers stretching him open from the inside, the long digits coated generously in saliva, easing their passage. "Yes, oh gods, oh *yes*, please . . ."

"Shen-Fei, let me see you when I—"

"No! It's not necessary, just hurry up and—"

"I *am* hurrying, I just don't want to hurt you," Sai-Jun snapped.

"You won't, I don't care, just *do* it, please, Sai-Jun–" Shen-Fei was babbling, as desperate and needy as he probably sounded.

He felt the sharp, lancing pain as Sai-Jun gave in and did as he asked, but then the gradual lessening of it, the stiffness in his back receding, his spine relaxing. He breathed out, slowly, and pushed back to meet Sai-Jun, the shock of this most private of caresses fading into the background.

Then they fucked. Uncaring, unrelenting, even angrily,

almost. Perhaps Sai-Jun, too, was frustrated it had taken them this long.

When it was over—when Sai-Jun slowly pulled out and away, giving Shen-Fei space to breathe, staring at him, looking somehow perplexed—Shen-Fei closed his eyes. And although his legs were trembling beneath him, although he felt wrung out, exhausted suddenly, he snapped them open again when he felt Sai-Jun's touch on him, softly now.

"Are you all right?"

"I'm fine. Why do you ask?" Shen-Fei grinned, but at the same time, he glanced carefully down. The elaborately embroidered sleeves of his robe, over-heavy for the season, were rumpled, like the rest of his clothing, but they remained covering what they needed to. Just to be safe, he pulled them down further, the ends of the voluminous fabric reaching almost to the floor, covering not only his arms but half of his hands.

"Here. Let me help—"

"*No.*"

They both froze at the word, Sai-Jun looking first bewildered, then annoyed, Shen-Fei trying not to show his fear. There was a long silence.

"Well." Sai-Jun's voice was suddenly much cooler. "This was clearly a . . . misjudgment on my part. I apologize. Sincerely. It will not happen again."

Shen-Fei took a step back, startled by the iciness in his tone. "I didn't mean—"

"It's fine," came the short reply. "These things happen, I suppose. But I should not have been so indiscreet. It was my mistake."

Each word was another blow, as sharp and precise as a needle. *Mistake.* "Oh. I didn't realize you felt that way."

Gods, but he'd been stupid beyond belief. Of *course* Shen-Fei had mistaken a little friendliness, a little sexual tension, entirely natural between men of their age and physical prox-imity, for true desire. Even among those who had known him for years, studied directly alongside him, Sai-Jun was known to be notoriously standoffish. And now Shen-Fei had com-pletely blown any chance he had of growing closer by dis-playing his own desperation, casting aside his dignity — something which, to someone like Sai-Jun, was no doubt one of the most sacred virtues a man could possess.

Overcome with embarrassment that bordered on self-dis-gust, Shen-Fei snorted at the thought. "I guess I should be on my way, then." Even so, he tried to disguise the hurt in his voice, and was relieved to hear the words sounded perfectly nonchalant. As if he had not just hitched up his robes and al-lowed himself, face pressed against the wall, to be taken like the cheapest of whores.

"By all means." Sai-Jun waved a hand. "Please, go on ahead. You know where the door is."

Glaring now in an effort to hold back his tears, Shen-Fei nodded, the movement stiff. Then, in an act he knew was sheer pettiness, but somehow unable to stop himself, he bowed low, formally, his words heavy with sarcasm. "Spir-itual Advisor."

He didn't look back even once as he strode from the room, so as not to give Sai-Jun the satisfaction of seeing the tears overflow.

CHAPTER ONE

The doors to the garden leading from the private audience hall were slid open to allow in fresh air from the small garden beyond, but no breeze stirred.

Inside the almost empty hall, Sai-Jun, spiritual advisor to the lord of the province of Foshana, kneeled on a richly embroidered cushion opposite his master. Despite the oppressive heat and lack of any formal audience, for none but his lord's servants were in attendance, Sai-Jun still wore his formal black robes, the color of his office. Beads of sweat gathered at the nape of his neck, but he did not fidget.

"And the distribution of talismans, my lord?" he asked. "As you well know, the townsfolk have extraordinarily long memories. I recommend allowing the townspeople to collect their talismans early this year, lest the more superstitious among them start to wonder. Your father, may his soul rest in the arms of the gods, made this mistake in his time, and given the drought and subsequent famine that followed . . ." Sai-Jun's voice trailed off, seeing that his lord was plainly not listening, but instead glancing listlessly around at the empty hall. Sai-Jun cleared his throat pointedly. "My lord?"

Still his master did not attend him, and Sai-Jun, knowing perfectly well that his lord's words were as law, could not resist the temptation. Expression carefully blank, he muttered several words under his breath and placed his palm softly on the ground, fingers splayed wide. His lord jumped, an undignified curse echoing throughout the hall, at the jolt of energy that flickered from the tips of his softly-shoed feet and up through the rest of his body—not enough to hurt, of course, but just the right amount to bring his attention back where it was warranted.

Now Lord Han-Zi attended. He scowled. "What was that for?"

"You weren't listening. My lord."

Han-Zi sighed. "It's hot. I don't know how you can stand to wear those ridiculous robes."

Sai-Jun waited.

" . . . And I scarcely know what you've been speaking of for the last half hour," his lord admitted, though he did not look particularly sorry.

Sai-Jun bowed from the waist without shifting his posture, glancing toward the servant who sat a discreet distance away, parchment and quill still at the ready. He, too, looked uncomfortable in the stifling hall.

"Which is why I took pains to ensure everything is being recorded, my lord. You will be able to read all the details at your leisure."

Han-Zi's scowl deepened. "I could have you hanged for daring to use magic against your lord," he complained, though both men knew he would do no such thing, nor even consider it. Supreme ruler of the province and a decade Sai-Jun's senior Han-Zi might be, but their relationship was closer to friends than master and servant. Besides, unlike his father before him, Han-Zi was never one to stand on ceremony, and in fact was constantly admonishing Sai-Jun to relax a little more, and not take his office—or indeed, life—so seriously.

"Perhaps my lord would care for a cool drink?" Without bothering to ask leave, Sai-Jun beckoned his master's body servants forward. One rushed over to Han-Zi with a lacquered cup, another with a flask of chilled water. When they had finished serving their lord, they approached Sai-Jun, who shook his head and gestured them away.

One year into his post as spiritual advisor, and the prestige this brought him still made him uncomfortable. Especially during such informal occasions, he preferred to serve himself when necessary, not have strangers fuss over him as though he were some lord or visiting dignitary. In fact, he owned no land nor title save for what his natural abilities and years of study had earned him, and his parents were naught but farmers in a far-flung village, many hours from the capital. He did not think he would ever grow completely used to being served by others.

Han-Zi sighed appreciatively as he sipped from his cup, then raised an eyebrow at the unmoving Sai-Jun. "Gods, it makes me uncomfortable just to look at you. How can you even breathe in those things? You needn't have worn your formal robes to this meeting at all, you know. I've told you time and time again—"

"Yes, my lord. But as this meeting concerns official business, I felt it only right to dress appropriately. Now, as I was saying, the talismans . . ."

A small head poked in through the doorway from the garden, and Han-Zi's expression lightened immediately, his attention once more stolen. "Little scamp! Don't think I don't see you there! Now why on earth is your face so dirty?"

The young boy's face was indeed quite filthy, smeared with grime and somewhat damp, through his grin was triumphant. "It was a mighty battle, father! I won."

"Naturally." Han-Zi laughed. "Come here then, young warrior." His son, recently turned six years of age, darted over, heedless of the mud from the shallow pond outside falling to the polished wooden floor in soggy clumps.

Sai-Jun gave a world-weary sigh, knowing the moment was lost. However, it was difficult to fault Han-Zi for being such a doting father, even if he did at times wish his lord would be a little less prone to distraction.

"We shall finish later then, my lord." Sai-Jun stood, ignoring the pain in his knees from where he had been kneeling, and gave a formal bow.

"I am sorry, Sai-Jun." To his credit, Han-Zi did sound genuinely apologetic. "Have your scribe deliver the notes to my chambers. I will study them, I promise. Today," he added when Sai-Jun continued to gaze at him unblinkingly.

"Of course, my lord."

Sai-Jun turned and made for the door, turning once more to bow before exiting as was proper, although the gesture was entirely lost on Han-Zi, who was now busy tickling his son and ignoring the mud staining his own costly robes in the process. A peel of childish laughter heralded Sai-Jun's departure.

Outside, the long maze of halls was somewhat cooler, the windows on either side thrown open to let in as much air as possible. He passed watchful guards standing at attention in their brown leather armor, as well as several servants going quietly about their duties, most clad in the dove-gray colors signifying that they served directly under Han-Zi and not another noble or palace advisor. Sai-Jun continued briskly on to his own work rooms, steps echoing slightly, his thoughts once again on the various tasks ahead of him for the day, then to what he had been speaking of with Han-Zi.

Every year, the palace created special talismans, providing these to the heads of every household in the capital of Foshana. Adhering to centuries of tradition, the talismans were to be hung at the entrance of every man's home as a token to the gods. Upon moving across the sky as the hot season drew to a close, the gods were said to glimpse these talismans on their journey and remember to bless the land with enough rain over the next several weeks for the crops to grow.

Organization of this yearly tradition fell to the palace's spiritual advisor, one who was marked by the gods to carry out such work—and as Sai-Jun had taken over the post just under a year ago, when his elderly master had passed on and the rainy season had already begun, this was Sai-Jun's first year overseeing the responsibility.

Like every other task given to him, Sai-Jun was determined to see it done properly. When his abilities to act as a conduit for the gods had made themselves known as a young child and he had been moved to the capital, he had studied the histories for years as part of his training, and he knew full well what might happen if traditions were not upheld and disaster happened to strike. It was as he had informed Han-Zi — many of the townspeople were highly superstitious, and in the worst of cases, blame at refusing to follow age-old customs could eventually lead to bloodshed.

Musing on such thoughts, his mind fully occupied, Sai-Jun strolled through the veritable labyrinth of the palace corridors. Then, rounding a corner, he all but collided with a face he knew well.

"Sorry, sorry, I'm — oh. It's you."

He looks thinner than when I last saw him. Sai-Jun repressed the thought. "Shen-Fei. Take care where you walk." His voice came out more curtly than he'd intended. But then, it usually did when it came to addressing Shen-Fei.

"You're the one who bumped into me!"

"Perhaps if you had not been walking so fast, I would not have," Sai-Jun pointed out. "Though walking might be something of an understatement, I see."

Shen-Fei flushed. From his rumpled appearance and still heavy breathing, it was obvious that he had been near-running — a clear breach of protocol. Servants rushed when their lords and ladies summoned them. Townsfolk rushed about their errands in the market. Lords and their offspring — particularly high-ranking ones — were too decorous to rush anywhere, even when pressed for time. But perhaps Shen-Fei was merely red from the heat. Certainly his robes, with their heavy trailing sleeves, were not at all suitable for such oppressively hot weather. His fussy, even ostentatious manner of dress, adopted at some point during his adolescence, had always struck Sai-Jun as strange, for the general's son did not otherwise seem like someone who cared all that much for outward appearances. As a child, he certainly never had—and for a brief moment, Sai-Jun recalled that grinning boy, a little brash and outspoken but always kind, with a deft hand for brush and ink, sketching surprisingly delicate figures of animals when he should have been paying heed to his lessons. *Where did that boy go?*

Sai-Jun realized he had been staring. Shen-Fei was still eyeing him angrily, no doubt taking Sai-Jun's silence as a personal affront to his already frayed dignity. Sai-Jun arched an eyebrow, waiting.

" . . . I was looking for my father," Shen-Fei finally said. "He was in the training courtyard just a while ago. I don't suppose you've seen him?"

"No," Sai-Jun replied shortly. "I have no business with the general." *Nor do I hope to.* He refrained from speaking this last, but the words hung soundlessly in the air around them, nonetheless. Though it would be blatant rudeness to say so, Sai-Jun and General Shen-Ya had never enjoyed one another's company.

For whatever reason, Shen-Fei's face grew redder, and he suddenly looked down at the ground as though it fascinated him. Then, still without looking Sai-Jun in the eye, he offered a hasty bow and passed him by without another word.

Half exasperated, half mystified, Sai-Jun permitted himself a sigh and continued on his way, attempting without success to bring his unruly thoughts back to his daily tasks.

Once safely back in his rooms near the opposite end of the palace, small but neat, and tucked away from the hustle and bustle of most of the rest of the palace, he finally discarded his heavy black robe and sat cross-legged on a cushion before his work desk, closing his eyes to better still his mind. There was much to be done before the day was through—he would accomplish nothing by dwelling on the past, or on Shen-Fei . . . though the mere thought of the young man's father, the general of Foshana, had him clenching his jaw. No, they had never once liked one another, and the fact that he of all people was father to Shen-Fei made it ten times worse.

Sai-Jun had always felt that although they were technically now of equal rank given their respective positions on the council, General Shen-Ya looked down on him, both for his youth and his humble family lineage, scoffing at any suggestion he made and refusing to give Sai-Jun any more courtesy than was strictly necessary for appearance's sake.

For his part, Sai-Jun loathed Shen-Ya just as much, if not more so, in return, for all he had to admit that the general did his job well and was without doubt one of the best fighters in the province, to say nothing of being a keen strategist. Lord Han-Zi awarded council positions based largely on merit, not merely upbringing or tradition, and had never been one to suffer fools as his advisors. Nonetheless, the general had a cruel streak that Sai-Jun instinctively disapproved of, though it was not his place to say so. He had seen Shen-Ya lash out at his servants for the slightest of honest mistakes. If Sai-Jun only had the power to remove him from his office . . .

No matter. He did not have that power, and it was none of his business anyway. Nor was Shen-Fei, and nor would he ever be. *Again.*

Now exasperated at himself more than anyone else, Sai-Jun abandoned his poor attempt at meditation, instead moving closer to his desk, where he snatched up a piece of blank parchment and his quill. If meditation failed to take his mind off matters that did not concern him, hard work surely would.

Dipping his quill into the nearby pot of ink, Sai-Jun began to write out a list of those things that needed preparing for the creation of the talismans he had been speaking of earlier to Han-Zi, still trying — and still failing miserably — to banish the general's son from his thoughts.

CHAPTER TWO

"Father?" Shen-Fei spoke hesitantly, leaning forward from where he kneeled at the low table. "Perhaps we should leave . . . I—"

The general barely spared his son a glance. "We leave when I say we leave, no sooner." He eyed his still half-filled goblet with some distaste. However, when one of the other tavern patrons, this one heavily muscled and seated a few feet away at another table, looked his way and bowed in recognition, Shen-Ya gave a gracious nod in return, draining the wine in a moment, before raising a hand to a passing tavern servant to order another.

As a child, Shen-Fei had thought it odd that his father would choose to frequent such places around the city, when at home—even with wine of far better quality than any could expect to find in a public drinking house—he rarely drank at all. Moreover, if he did, it was very rarely to excess. Shen-Ya possessed an iron-clad self-control that never seemed to relax, even in private company. Now a young man, his son knew the truth of it—Shen-Ya thought it important to be seen among the common people, especially the soldiers under his command, and enjoyed the popularity this brought him.

"Our general is one of us," his men commonly boasted among themselves. "A noble who could be supping on the best of wines offered to him by bowing servants, yet still not too lofty to fraternize with his own. Now *there's* a real warrior for you."

And indeed, among those in his charge, Shen-Ya was

mostly well-liked, known as someone who would push his soldiers hard, demanding perfection, yet honoring their work and achievements by drinking alongside them rather than spending his leisure time secluded in the comfort of his luxurious townhouse, barely a stone's throw from the palace. The general's deeply sun-browned skin and heavily calloused hands reinforced the image not of a cosseted aristocrat — though his lineage was undeniably noble — but of someone who was never too proud to practice his own teachings.

Shen-Fei glanced down at his own empty goblet, knowing he had fulfilled his filial duties enough that he might retreat without offering offense — publicly, at least. His father would be displeased, but tongues would not wag that Shen-Fei had disrespected the general by refusing to drink with him. He bowed and rose from his cushion, mumbling something about the heat — true enough, for in the dimly lit tavern, the air was stifling — and caught the unmistakable look of irritation his father directed at him before his escape, though Shen-Ya deigned to say nothing.

Outside, it was still hot, though the air was at least fresher. Shen-Fei loitered a moment by the entrance — should he wait here for his father to finish? But that could be hours yet, especially if the general began circulating the tavern as he sometimes did, greeting his soldiers and talking with them as they liked, pretending interest as he asked after their wives and children. What kind of image would that make, the son of the general waiting alone outside a tavern like a dog for his master? Tongues would most certainly wag then, and his father would be even less pleased than he was already.

Fingering a slight bruise on his cheekbone, Shen-Fei winced at the thought. No, better to leave for home and await his father there. Then he could deliver the message that he dared not give in public, which had found Shen-Fei while he had been earlier alone in the house save for the servants — that all of Lord Han-Zi's closest advisors and top-ranking officials had been called to council one month from now.

This was a significant occasion, as Lord Han-Zi made public many important decisions during this meeting, which in times of peace was held but once a year. Such decisions would impact every sphere of the governance of Foshana, both financially and militarily. Shen-Fei had never attended such a meeting and would not unless he succeeded his father as general or was awarded some other high advisory role, but he knew it would also include lesser decisions, yet ones especially noteworthy on a more individual basis, from promotions to arranged marriages. Once decisions were officially declared in council, the general public would also be informed of such things, which would then become an immediate subject of gossip in the days and weeks that followed. Depending on who you were and how you felt you had performed over the previous year — whether you had distinguished yourself in the eyes of your superiors or committed acts worthy of reward — people either looked forward to or dreaded this annual call to council, whose date was only ever declared a month in advance, since by tradition, it always occurred just before the change of the seasons, from mercilessly hot to torrential rain. Only days after this, likewise by long-held tradition, the heads of every household in the capital would be summoned to the palace to collect their talismans, hanging these at the outdoor entranceways of their homes to pray for the rain that should arrive shortly afterward. This ceremony was always overseen by one particular member of the council — the spiritual advisor of Foshana itself.

Shen-Fei swallowed. This year, that role would be fulfilled for the first time by Sai-Jun. He was probably busy preparing even now, meticulously ensuring that all preparations would be in place when the time came. Even as a child, Sai-Jun had always been diligent — Shen-Fei remembered this all too well from their palace studies together. And now, not even a full year older than Shen-Fei, his diligence had paid off, and he was the youngest spiritual advisor to hold the post in the last one hundred years.

"Master Shen-Fei!" In his musings, he had already neared his father's holdings, where the servants busy in the lavish outdoor garden took notice and bowed. "Welcome home, sir."

Shen-Fei allowed himself to smile and gesture a somewhat casual greeting in return — something he took care never to do in the company of Shen-Ya. If his father was popular with his soldiers, Shen-Fei was popular among their household servants, who often took the brunt of Shen-Ya's anger and tended to tiptoe about whenever they were in his presence, lest they incite his rage for whatever error or misdemeanor, imagined or otherwise. A few had been employed in this home for years, and remembered Shen-Fei's mother, the Lady Mei, with great fondness — Shen-Fei had heard the older servants whisper of her more than the once. Though a sickly woman, she had always treated all of the members of the household with kindness, and up until her death, had never been prone to the same outbursts as her husband, even as her body grew frail and wracked with the pain of her illness.

"Young master, will the general be following shortly?" asked the servant who removed Shen-Fei's shoes and his outer robe once he entered the inner residence.

"I think not," Shen-Fei replied, and averted his eyes so as not to see the servant's shoulders drop in unseemly relief. It was not proper to allow such disrespect to remain unpunished, especially as the general's own son — but at least he need not feel shame at what he did not see. And out of necessity, there was much in the general's household to which he and many of the servants were intentionally blind.

Later that night, sitting silently at the low table as the servants brought dinner, kneeling on padded cushions embroidered in red with their family crest, Shen-Fei eyed his father warily.

When, upon Shen-Ya's return, his son had handed him the message about the date of the council, Shen-Ya had taken the note bearing Lord Han-Zi's official seal, nodded, and swept to his rooms without a word, his face inscrutable. Whether he approved or not, anticipated good news or bad, no one could tell. Now darkness was falling and the food nearly all consumed, and still he had uttered barely a word, to his son or anyone else.

Unaccountably nervous, Shen-Fei fidgeted, then glanced around for something, anything, innocuous to say to break the tense quiet.

Scarlet tapestries decorated the walls about them — the general's colors, red for blood, so that on the battlefield, their enemies should not see if they managed to draw any. The stone foundations of the house had been smoothed out, and costly rugs lay here and there on the fastidiously polished wooden floors. As a child at least, Shen-Fei had not minded the bright splashes of color, but tonight, they seemed overly intense, even garish. He felt a dull pulsing in his temples — the beginnings of a headache. Would it be so bad, he wondered, to display some other prominent color in the house? A cooler shade, perhaps, or simply something less bright, that did not have to constantly remind of war or bloodshed? Even a very simple color, one that promised a calming strength, like . . .

"Black," he found himself whispering to himself.

"What's that?"

"N-nothing, Father."

What would Sai-Jun think if he saw such blood-red decorations surrounding him? Most likely curl his lip, Shen-Fei decided. The spiritual advisor's own color was black — symbolic

17

of the mysterious yet sacred power bestowed on one marked by the gods, and reserved for those who were blessed as such. It suited him, for Sai-Jun had always been one to eschew ostentatious symbols of rank and seemed to dislike anything that brought undue attention. When they had studied together, the sons or apprentices of nobility and important advisors receiving the highest forms of education in the palace while their elders went about their duties elsewhere, Sai-Jun had always been among the quietest and most hardworking of students. He'd also, Shen-Fei remembered, produced the most beautiful calligraphy he had ever seen. The dark ink flowed across the page boldly, elegantly, making even the most mundane of copied scripture beautiful to look at. It seemed almost inevitable that Sai-Jun would now wear black as well. It matched his near-equally dark gaze and made his skin appear even more dramatically pale by comparison. Did the man ever venture outside, or did he remain cooped up in the palace always, a silent figure sweeping through the halls? Did he not ever miss the sun? Did he never grow lonely?

"Wake up, boy!" The table jostled as a hand slammed down upon the smoothed wooden surface, and Shen-Fei forced himself not to flinch. Weakness was not tolerated — not on the battlefield, and not here in the general's own home. "Call the servants, and do not make me ask a third time!"

"Y-yes, Father."

Shen-Fei moved to call the servants back into the room to clear their plates and bring the last of their meal. Son obeyed father — so it was, and so it always would be in the kingdom, the natural order of things — no matter what anyone, least of all Shen-Fei, might wish.

"They are coming, Father."

As two servants entered quietly, one to clean and one to carry, Shen-Fei watched without really seeing as they went about their duties, neither daring to speak nor even to swap sympathetic looks with him as they occasionally did, despite the risk this entailed.

Shen-Ya watched too, but his gaze was razor-sharp, and Shen-Fei only just refrained from breathing an audible sigh of relief when they left the room again without drawing rebuke.

One way or another, they were all trapped.

CHAPTER THREE

Sai-Jun stood in front of his lord once more and made his customary bow. "My lord, preparations for the ceremony are progressing smoothly. I anticipate no troubles, provided my interpretations of the auguries were correct. I believe them to be so — the rains should not begin until several days later."

Han-Zi nodded and waved a hand, indicating Sai-Jun could dispense with the formalities if he wished. "You've done well, as usual. Indeed, nobody could find fault with your work. You are fastidious as always."

Sai-Jun bowed again. "I bask in my lord's praise." A slightly exasperated sigh greeted these words, and Sai-Jun looked up at the sound. "My lord?"

"We are alone — surely you can unbend enough to speak to me as the friend you are? And speaking of which . . ."

Sai-Jun inwardly sighed, having a feeling that he knew what was coming.

" . . . It troubles me that you labor so hard yet seemingly care so little for your own welfare," Han-Zi continued. "In fact, my servants say you're often among the first to rise in the morning and among the last to bed at night. Do you plan on working yourself to death?"

Sai-Jun almost rolled his eyes at this clear exaggeration, but kept his expression stubbornly neutral. "I am spiritual advisor, my lord. It is expected of me, and I do not begrudge my work."

"Even so, surely you must wish for something more?" Han-Zi pressed. "Some recompense for your efforts?

Especially given your youth. Since the council is approaching . . ."

"My lord?" Sai-Jun asked again, this time in genuine confusion. "My position is more than recompense—especially, as you say, at such a young age. The honor is more than enough—certainly I could ask for nothing more than—"

"I did not mean riches," Han-Zi interrupted. "There is of course no urgency, but . . . well, do you not wish to be wed? Most other ranking advisors have wives to greet them when they return from their duties, and many of them, children to brighten their days of freedom, even those who choose to reside permanently in the palace apartments provided for their work. Those who are marked by the gods may choose to spend their lives alone, even as your predecessor did, but your role as spiritual advisor does not require you to be chaste, as well you know. You are no monk or temple priest. Should you wish, it is not yet too late for me to arrange something so that it can be made official in this year's council. There are many unwed women from good families who I have no doubt would look highly on such a match—not only beautiful, for I know you do not care only for outward appearances, but also kind, diligent, with virtue and intelligence to match your own—"

"Please, I beg you." Sai-Jun spoke quietly but emphatically. "I do not . . . your generosity is unparalleled, but I have no wish to take a wife. None at all," he pressed. He chose not to elaborate on his words.

There was a brief silence, surprise showing briefly on Han-Zi's face, followed by a barely restrained grin. "Ah. You already have somebody on your mind."

"No!" Sai-Jun spoke too quickly, and the smile on his lord's face grew. "No," said Sai-Jun again, quieter this time. "You mistake my meaning. I am simply too busy with my work to give any woman the attention she would deserve. My lord."

He strove to return to his previous formality, but he was rattled, and Han-Zi clearly knew it.

"Sai-Jun . . ." Han-Zi's expression grew more mischievous as his lord appeared to remember something. "Do you recollect the evening it was formally announced that you would take over the office of spiritual advisor?"

Sai-Jun felt his posture instinctively stiffen, but managed to keep his voice perfectly even. "Of course, my lord."

"It was a most celebratory occasion. I do not believe I had ever seen you so . . . gregarious in manner."

"As you say, my lord, it was a celebratory occasion." He dared not meet his lord's gaze now, instead focusing on a point near Han-Zi's shoulder.

"I seem to recall . . ." Han-Zi's hand moved to stroke his beard, clearly enjoying every moment of his friend's discomfiture. " . . . You were getting along rather well with the general's son . . . young Shen-Fei, yes? You are of an age, I believe, and if memory serves, you studied alongside one another for some years as peers here in the palace."

"It all seems so long ago," Sai-Jun murmured, noncommittally. "I barely recall those days."

"Indeed? Yet it was only a year ago — less, in fact — when the two of you seemed rather close. Sai-Jun."

"Yes, my lord?"

"You disappeared later on that same celebratory evening. As did Shen-Fei. Is it not so?"

Sai-Jun cursed his lord's long memory. "I . . . could not say for certain, my lord. The wine . . ." He made a vague gesture, flustered.

"No? Well, I could."

Sudden anger filled him. Sai-Jun had done his best, his very best, to forget that night entirely — and until fairly recently, he had been succeeding. What gave anyone the right, even one in such a position of power as Lord Han-Zi, to poke his nose into Sai-Jun's personal affairs? He was not obligated to account for his choices in bed partners . . . had anyone been such. And they had not. They had *not*. What had occurred that night nearly a year ago now was simply . . . a young man's folly, his mind fogged with drink. He had admitted as such to Shen-Fei, who for his part had rushed out the door as soon as that shameful act had come to a finish. What right had Han-Zi to drag this back up again after all this time?

"My lord," Sai-Jun bit off. "I respect your authority — and your powers of recollection — but I assure you, you could not be more off the mark. My relationship with Shen-Fei — such as it is — is strictly impersonal. As you say, we studied alongside each other as peers. That is all."

"Don't be ridiculous," Han-Zi scoffed. "Do you really think I haven't noticed your mind has been elsewhere of late, even as you go about your work with remarkable diligence? What occurred that night is hardly a well-kept secret, at least among those who attended the celebration. Surely you do not truly intend to allow your dislike for the father to keep you from happiness with the son — "

"I have no feelings for Shen-Fei!" Sai-Jun's voice echoed around the audience chamber. Composure thoroughly broken, knowing full well his lord must be enjoying every minute of this, he continued heatedly. "And how, pray tell, is it that you know of my dislike for Shen-Ya? Do you have spies follow me throughout the palace, recording my every comment?"

"Of course not." Han-Zi seemed not only entirely unphased by Sai-Jun's angry outburst, but even almost glad of it. "You *are* young, my friend. Only a fool would not be able to see your enmity for the general. You may think yourself outwardly impassive — and be assured, you are, for the most part — but I am lord of this province, and I know well enough that my advisors do not always get along. Such is to be expected. I require first and foremost that anyone playing a role in my council be the most competent man for the job. This often necessitates strong personalities. People sometimes butt heads." He waved a hand dismissively. "This is only natural. But so be it. You wish to speak of other topics?" His gaze became more intense. "It is my responsibility to ensure that such hostilities do not hinder anyone's work. What have you against Shen-Ya?"

"My lord . . ." Reflexively, Sai-Jun glanced around, though the chamber was empty save for the lord's own servants, all of whom he knew to be steadfastly loyal and sworn to silence. Not even a scribe was in attendance today.

"You may speak freely," Han-Zi said, seeing Sai-Jun's restless gaze. "And so you should, since this potentially affects not only you and Shen-Ya, but the entire upcoming council as well. So. Speak, and know I will not judge you. We speak now not as lord and subject, but friend to friend. What has Shen-Ya done to offend you so?"

Sai-Jun sighed, knowing he was defeated before he even began. "Nothing at all, my lord. That is . . . nothing I may point to. None could argue that the general carries out his duties to the best of his abilities. He is a master strategist and a warrior such as any lord could be proud of to lead his armies." He frowned, attempting to convey his feelings into words. "It's just . . ."

Han-Zi rested his chin in his hands, waiting.

"It's instinct, my lord. Perhaps general and spiritual advisor would never see eye to eye at the best of times, given their disparate roles—I freely admit, I am no warrior. Moreover, the general and I were raised in very different ways of life. But I say to you honestly, I see something in him I do not like. Worse, I see something in him I despise," he admitted frankly. "My lord must know that Shen-Ya is hardly a man of benign temperament."

"That much is true enough," Han-Zi acknowledged. "But have a care, Sai-Jun. If you have no action to accuse him of, no reason for your feelings but instinct . . . well. You are young, as we've both established. And you may trust me, if you trust no other to say so, that it will do you no good to appear at odds with Shen-Ya without good reason. He is an influential man, both in public and in the council, as well you know. I can protect your position. I can do little when it comes to your personal life. There are all sorts of ways a man like that could make it a miserable one if he so chose. Think on this."

Sai-Jun was silent for a moment. Then, schooling his expression and his voice back to neutrality, he finally spoke again. "You are saying for yourself he is dangerous, then."

Han-Zi returned Sai-Jun's look with an uncharacteristically serious one of his own. "When it comes to internal politics, *everyone* is dangerous, Sai-Jun. You would do well to remember that." Then his expression lightened a little. "All I am saying, of course, is to be careful who you side against—again, that's my advice not as your lord, but as a friend, and I pray you take it to heart. Don't give Shen-Ya, or anyone else for that matter, reason to hate you unless there truly is no better choice."

Sai-Jun gave a half-smile. "I fear it is too late for that. The man has made his own dislike of me quite clear. And when it comes to internal politics, I have no doubt that many more people besides Shen-Ya are caught up in them, albeit perhaps unwillingly."

"You speak of Shen-Fei?"

Sometimes Sai-Jun cursed his lord's apparent ability to read minds whenever it suited him, especially when he often made an outward show of offhandedness, perhaps even carelessness. Still, his lord—and yes, his friend, despite his infuriating meddling ways—was clearly doing his best to care for Sai-Jun's wellbeing, however much some of his comments rankled.

"Let us merely hope that the qualities of the father have not yet been given a chance to pass over to the son," Sai-Jun finally said, attempting to inject some lightness into his own voice.

Han-Zi laughed a little at this. "Really, you judge too hastily, Sai-Jun. I seem to remember the boy being as kind as his mother was—and though you did not have the opportunity to know her, I assure you, a kinder woman would have been difficult to find. But I have no doubt you would know better than I the character of Shen-Fei, hm?"

Realizing too late that he had given Han-Zi an all-too-easy opening, Sai-Jun bowed, his face studiously blank once again, and quickly took his leave—before his lord could think of another teasing remark to direct to him about that damnable Shen-Fei.

CHAPTER FOUR

The days passed by unrelentingly hot, as it always was before the rains finally began. The closer it grew to the change in weather, the more stifling the days and even the nights grew.

Shen-Fei sweated heavily as he left the large training grounds directly outside the palace, wishing he could at least strip himself of the close-fitting garments he wore beneath his outer robe, but unwilling to do so until he returned home for the day. For now, the shade offered by one of the palace's viewing balconies would have to do, from where he could watch as others of his father's men took their turn in hand-to-hand combat practice. Truly, it was a fiercely hot day for such activities—and if he must train, Shen-Fei would have much preferred to practice other skills, such as archery—but the other men endured their orders with little complaint. Needless to say, the general, who sweated alongside the rest, was as impassive as always, refusing to let his iron-clad control slip even an inch. Shen-Fei saw his father's mouth tighten, almost imperceptibly, as he watched Shen-Fei retreat into the shade, but there was no help for it. At least Shen-Fei had lasted throughout the morning, and he judged it was at least not unseemly to retire for a few moments.

So thinking, he made his way into the nearest palace entrance and up the polished stone steps, still breathing heavily but glad to be alone for now. However, his heart sank as he reached the top of the stairway and saw a black-robed figure already there, leaning on the balcony and gazing out over the training yard. It was too late to beat a hasty retreat—Sai-Jun was already turning at the sound of Shen-Fei's none-too-silent approach.

"What are you doing here?" Shen-Fei blurted out gracelessly. His face burned in embarrassment as well as with the heat now—why did he always have to be so awkward, especially when Sai-Jun was so collected? The man had probably never once lost his composure in his life.

"That is none of your concern," came the cool response. Then Sai-Jun sighed and seemed to reconsider. Resting beside him was a silver flagon of water, and he pushed this closer to Shen-Fei. "Drink. You look thirsty."

It would have been unthinkably impolite to refuse. Shen-Fei nodded stiffly and accepted the flagon. He hesitated, then poured some water into the only cup that sat alongside it, lifting it to his lips. The shock of the coolness of the water was an intense relief, almost dizzying him.

"I thank you."

"It is nothing." Sai-Jun was no longer even looking at him.

Following his gaze, Shen-Fei looked down at the fenced-off ring below them, where two men sparred under the direction of his father, who watched with seeming impassiveness as they practiced throwing one another to the ground, again and again until Shen-Ya declared himself satisfied. A different pair of men followed at the general's sharp gesture.

"I didn't know you liked to watch the fighting," Shen-Fei commented eventually, feeling the silence growing heavy.

"I was here already, taking some fresh air. The men just happened to begin practicing below."

That meant he had probably seen Shen-Fei spar. Hand-to-hand combat had never been his forte, and his father never shied away from reminding him of it. Oh, he could wield a sword with enough competency so as not to cause embarrassment, and he was more than competent with bow and arrow, but Shen-Fei had never taken to wrestling or fist-fighting, and knew he was considered the weaker for it. He wished his father would simply give up on him, but it seemed the general had hopes for his son yet, despite his lack of natural aptitude for fighting.

Shen-Fei looked down at his hands, unsure how to reply.

"You prefer archery, yes?" Sai-Jun continued.

Shen-Fei glanced up, the surprise clear in his voice. "How did you know?"

A shrug. "I didn't, really. Just a guess."

"That's some guess," Shen-Fei pressed.

"I am spiritual advisor, after all." Sai-Jun's face was as blank as ever.

"I didn't know mind reading was among the spiritual advisor's many talents." This came out more sarcastically than Shen-Fei had intended, and Sai-Jun frowned.

"And I did not know my *talents* were any of your concern."

Shen-Fei threw his hands up in defeat. "Fine, I'll take the hint. I leave you to your fresh air." He spun around and turned to leave.

"Wait!" A hand gripped his wrist. "Stay. I did not mean . . ."

"Let go of me!" Shen-Fei jerked his hand back, the movement stronger than intended. There came the sound of ripping material as part of his lower sleeve gave, revealing the tight-fitting black garment underneath.

"Apologies. I did not—"

"It's fine. It's fine." Shen-Fei was half reassuring himself. His heart hammered painfully. A close call.

"You're sweating," Sai-Jun observed.

"It's just the heat."

"You don't look well." The spiritual advisor's voice betrayed a hint of concern, which under other circumstances, might have been almost laughable.

29

As it was, Shen-Fei felt the world waver slightly around him as he sucked in a breath. "A touch of the sun. It will pass."

"Here . . ." Sai-Jun's hand supported his back as he led Shen-Fei a few steps away to where he could lean against the wall. "You're not dressed appropriately for such a day. How you can even think to train in such a heavy robe, and atop such close-fitting garments—"

"I said it's nothing!" He batted Sai-Jun's hands away and watched as a strange look passed over Sai-Jun's face before it was replaced with the usual blank stare. If he didn't know better—which he *did*, Shen Fei told himself firmly—he would have sworn that expression had been one of hurt.

Silence followed once more as the two men sat side by side, determinedly not looking at one another. Finally, to Shen-Fei's surprise, it was Sai-Jun who eventually broke it. "Why is it you seem so determined to hold me at arm's length?"

"*Me?*" Shen-Fei could feel his mouth hanging open in shock. "What about you? You're the one who pushed me away, the one who insisted . . ." He swallowed. "Never mind. What's done is done, right? There's no point arguing about it, least of all with you."

"And what exactly is that supposed to mean?" Sai-Jun's tone was icy.

"Please. You never did like to argue—you were always one to walk away rather than have it out. *Now*, a whole year after we . . . after you walked off *again*—"

"I'm not the one who walked away!"

"I left when you told me to leave!" Shen-Fei defended heatedly.

"Oh, spare me! As I recall, you could barely *wait* to get out the door!"

"Ha! That was only because . . ." Sai-Jun waited, still glaring, as Shen-Fei trailed off, suddenly more uncomfortable than angry and unwilling to finish. "It doesn't matter now," he finally said, this time more quietly, forcing himself to an appearance of calm. "Can we not at least be civil to one another in passing? Is that so much to ask?"

"No. It's not." Sai-Jun stood. "If that's how you feel, I certainly have no intention of trying to change your mind. Stay here and recuperate from the heat if you will. This time, *I'll* be the one to leave."

His dismissive comment stung, far more than Shen-Fei wanted to admit even to himself. It wasn't fair. Sai-Jun wasn't being fair—not then, and not now. "Wait!" he snapped.

"*What?*" Sai-Jun turned, snarling, and his own anger took Shen-Fei aback. He didn't know that he'd ever seen the spiritual advisor look so rattled. As if to accompany his words, a gust of wind billowed around them, sweeping Shen-Fei's heavy, sweat-dampened hair back from his face. The wind died down again almost immediately, and just as suddenly did Sai-Jun's expression change. " . . . What. Is. This?" His dark eyes glittered with some other, more private emotion that made Shen-Fei shiver.

"What's what?"

"*This.*"

He felt the touch of Sai-Jun's fingers on the upper part of his forehead, previously covered by sweat-dampened hair. Then, as Sai-Jun pressed a little harder and Shen-Fei felt the slight flash of pain, he realized what the spiritual advisor was alluding to. "Nothing. It's nothing." He did his best to make his voice sound light, nonchalant.

"It's not *nothing*," Sai-Jun insisted. "No wonder your manner seemed off earlier—do you still feel dizzy now? A head wound like this—"

"Don't be ridiculous," Shen-Fei tried to laugh. "Hardly worth calling a wound—only a small bruise."

"It's not small."

"Accidents happen all the time in the training yard."

"Not unless someone goes out of their way to inflict real damage. Could that be called training?"

"As I said, accidents happen. I simply took a tumble."

"You fell on your *head?*"

"No! I mean, yes. I was too close to the wall. I banged my head against the wall."

"Really." Sai-Jun crossed his arms. "When? I did not see that happen while I was watching."

"It happened the day before."

"Shen-Fei." Sai-Jun stared at him. "I am no healer, but that bruise is a deep purple. It did not happen yesterday."

Shen-Fei looked away, unable now to meet Sai-Jun's intent gaze. "I . . ." He could not finish. Could not find the words he knew he should have to defend himself. To defend his honor in the face of an implied accusation.

The wind blew again, stirring the hems of both their robes. "The law may permit the head of the household to discipline those living within," Sai-Jun spoke at last. "Nowhere does it state that he may unfairly beat them."

"You think you know everything." This emerged in a near-whisper. Shen-Fei had not intended to say anything at all, and the bitterness he heard in his own voice surprised him.

"You think not? Well, like your father, I, too, hold a place on the council. And I may not have as many years of experience, I grant you that, but believe me when I say this. I know full well what kind of man Shen-Ya is."

"My father is . . ." Shen-Fei was now caught between an outright lie and a statement that would cause unthinkable dishonor to speak aloud. Maligning the head of one's own household was not simply ill-mannered — it was borderline treasonous. As surely as night must follow day, and on and on in the natural order of things, so too must the son respect and obey the father. Such had been the law for centuries, and to break it, or even to imply that it was unfair or undesirable, meant absolute disgrace.

"Your father is a man who would beat others into submission to satisfy his own anger," Sai-Jun finished for him. The matter-of-factness of his tone had Shen-Fei feeling ashamed. He knew he should argue against the statement. People sometimes killed for less insult.

But he could not argue it. There was the truth of the matter, plain and simple.

There was only one thing for it. "I'm leaving now," he said with forced politeness. "Good day, Spiritual Advisor." He bowed stiffly and turned his back on Sai-Jun — and this time, thankfully, Sai-Jun uttered not a word as Shen-Fei made his escape.

CHAPTER FIVE

Sai-Jun awoke with a start, only then realizing he had been dreaming.

He took a moment to reorient himself and wipe the sweat from his brow. The chamber was stifling, and his white sleep robes clung damply to his limbs. He began straightening the covers that had somehow twisted about him as he'd slept, then abandoned the effort and got up instead, not bothering to dress. He made his way over to his low work desk, kneeling on the cushion before it and quickly lighting a candle. The shadows danced and flickered over the walls.

Dreams, Sai-Jun knew from his studies, came in all manner of forms. Some meant nothing—near-irrelevant imaginings from the inner consciousness as the mind refreshed itself, allowing the body to follow. Other dreams might be more meaningful—these could come not only from within, but from other, external forces at work. When called upon, it was the job of the spiritual advisor to distinguish one type of dream from another, using both natural intuition and deep learning from years of study to determine what message they portended and why. Many times in the past, those in this role used their own dreams to foretell and prepare for unexpected or dangerous events, and even to prevent otherwise unpredicted tragedies such as illness or the death of important state figures, or the coming of natural disasters.

Sai-Jun hurried to grind fresh ink, instinct urging him to write his dream down before it faded from memory. There had been a snake slithering past his feet—that could mean either knowledge, or the lack of it. Something he needed to find out? Then, as the snake had continued on its way, a man had approached, cloaked and hooded. A mysterious figure, who likely symbolized someone Sai-Jun already knew, but who was either remaining hidden or hiding something important, intentionally or not. As the man drew nearer, his face still hidden in darkness, he had raised a hand, his sleeve falling back from his wrist to reveal a bare arm, seemingly patterned in some way by twisting shadows, these too almost snake-like. Secrets upon secrets. The figure stretched his arm out toward Sai-Jun in a gesture of . . . what? Warning? Entreaty? Diligently, Sai-Jun noted both of these possibilities down, the quill scratching quickly at the parchment. Finally, the mysterious person had pointed to the sky, and glancing upward, Sai-Jun saw lightning peel across it on an otherwise clear day. This part of the message was clear: dire consequences without action. Still, the fact that there had been nothing accompanying the lightning—no thunder or rain, nor even wind, usually meant to delay action in order to ensure the most advantageous outcome.

Sai-Jun pinched the bridge of his nose, feeling a headache coming on. Act quickly but wait? Sometimes, he thought to himself wryly, the art of dream interpretation was far more trouble than it was worth.

Knowing sleep would now be impossible, he continued to sit in silent thought as the chamber gradually lightened around him, the candle burning down and down as the minutes passed. Dawn eventually broke, and a chorus of birdsong from outside finally heralded the new day. Still Sai-Jun continued to sit, now in deep meditation, as the rest of the world began to awaken.

When he heard the light tread of a servant outside his rooms, followed by a respectful tap at the door, he opened his eyes again and knew, without quite knowing how, what he had to do.

First came action.

"Come in, Mishka." He spoke quietly, and the servant opened the door and approached. He bore Sai-Jun's usual morning drink, a steaming cup of tea made up of herbs that Sai-Jun had always found to sharpen the mind and banish any vestiges of sleep.

Mishka bowed and placed the tray and cup on the table. Familiar with his master's ways, he did not offer to assist Sai-Jun in dressing. "Have you any orders for the morning, sir?"

"Yes. We have a new servant among our ranks, do we not?"

Mishka nodded, surprise flitting across his face. "You mean Feng, sir? He replaced another servant a week ago after he was called to a family wedding on the outskirts of the province. Feng has been adept at his duties, sir. We have found no fault with him."

"Good, for I do not have punishment in mind. Send him to me, immediately."

"Sir." Mishka bowed and left, returning in several minutes with the new servant in tow, whose nervousness at being so abruptly summoned was written clearly on his face.

"Leave us now, Mishka, and attend to your duties freely. I would speak with Feng alone."

"Yes, sir." Mishka exited the chamber, sliding the door closed silently behind him.

At Sai-Jun's gesture, Feng kneeled in front of him. "Sir, if I have in some way given offense—"

Sai-Jun held up a hand. "As I informed Mishka, you are not here for punishment." Belatedly, he realized he was still clad in his somewhat rumpled sleeping robes, his long hair undressed and sleep tousled. Hardly decorous for a spiritual advisor—no wonder Feng seemed anxious. Never mind—he'd had more important things than his appearance to attend to.

"But I have need of your services now, as your face is still known only to a few," he continued. "I already know from Mishka that you are proficient in your duties. Tell me, do you also know how to be discreet?"

"Sir?" Feng's nervous look was now mixed with curiosity.

"I am about to request something . . . unusual from you. Highly unusual. You may of course refuse my request, as it lies well outside your usual requirements. It may also involve some danger. Rest assured, however, that if you should carry this out for me, I will be in your debt and find a way to repay you appropriately."

Feng bowed low, his forehead nearly brushing the floor. "I am your servant, sir. Whatever you ask of me, I will do my best to carry out my task." His sincerity was obvious, and Sai-Jun felt a rush of gratitude, although he knew it would be unseemly of him to show it.

"Very well. Understand that this is to remain entirely between us. No one else is to know — none of the other servants, even those in my own employ, no member of your own family. *Nobody.*"

"I understand, sir."

Sai-Jun nodded. "Very well. I shall not mince words. I wish you to go to General Shen-Ya's house this very day. Not now, for the general will soon be here at the palace conducting scheduled morning drills, if I am not mistaken. But after he returns home in the afternoon, you are to keep watch without being seen. Do not enter the home or speak to anyone. I am not asking you to look for anything . . . specific. I simply want to know what goes on there. If there is anything out of the ordinary, anything of note . . ." Sai-Jun shook his head, frustrated at himself. What good would this do? What had he to go on, other than a dream? "These instructions are hardly precise, I am well aware."

"I understand, sir." Feng was sitting up straight again, both

37

his posture and gaze intense. "How long should I remain there?"

Sai-Jun thought for a moment. "I trust to your judgment. If there is anything . . . strange, or noteworthy that occurs, come to find me immediately—I give you leave to interrupt whatever activity of mine that you must. If not, remain until you feel you can do so no longer—without risk of discovery or suspicion, of course. Above all, you must have a care for your own safety, but should you be apprehended or suspected of any wrongdoing, rest assured it is I who will take responsibility. Remember that."

"Yes, sir."

"Good . . . ah, your robes," Sai-Jun remembered, frowning.

"They are too conspicuous, sir." Feng caught on immediately.

"Good man." Feng was a quick study, and Sai-Jun gave an approving nod. All those who served directly under the spiritual advisor wore robes trimmed in black, making their position easily recognizable. "Ask one of the regular palace servants . . . no. Ask Mishka to ask one of the regular palace servants, someone whom he knows and trusts, to find him some spare plain gray servant's robes. Mishka will then deliver these to you. He will ask you no questions, and Mishka will know not to gossip to anyone else about such a request."

"Yes, sir."

"Go, then, and send Mishka back in. He will find you when it is time."

Feng bowed and swiftly left, and Sai-Jun got up and paced the room as he waited, now filled with a sense of trepidation. What were the chances, really, of anything happening that he could use to prevent this . . . whatever it was he felt the urge to stop? At this point, he was acting purely on instinct, even when logic told him that little could possibly come of this plan other than to waste his time, and that of his servants.

Moreover, if Feng was discovered spying, the consequences of Sai-Jun's actions would be far greater than a little embarrassment. It would bring shame upon his entire office, and he would likely have to account for his actions before not only Han-Zi, but the entire council.

But he was plotting a course now, and something held him from calling it off. Some deeper part of him — hopefully, the part that had landed him the role of spiritual advisor to begin with — whispered *good*.

And next?

Sai-Jun groaned, thinking about the following step he intuitively knew he needed to take.

Next came delay, for the council was scheduled to convene this very evening — and though he didn't himself yet know why, he could not allow that to take place. Not yet.

"My lord." Sai-Jun bowed deeply. He was wearing some of his most formal robes, hoping to impress upon Han-Zi the gravity of what he was about to ask.

Han-Zi was frowning, though more in bewilderment than annoyance. "What's amiss, Sai-Jun? I did not think we had any reason to hold a meeting between us this day — you assured me several days since that all was proceeding as planned. What has happened?"

"Nothing, my lord. At least, nothing yet. But I beg you to consider what I am about to say, no matter how unusual it may seem." He waited, barely breathing, for his lord's answer.

Han-Zi waved a hand. "You have your lord's ear. Speak."

Sai-Jun made no preamble. "I want you to delay the council."

Han-Zi's curious expression turned to one of shock. "Something must have happened indeed for you to suggest so. It would be highly unusual . . . the preparations are already underway, not to mention several of my advisors having traveled from their respective posts—"

"I know, my lord. Please, I implore you. It must not be held tonight."

"You can give me no reason? There must be *something*," he pressed. "I know you—you're not one to act impulsively."

"I . . . cannot offer any reason, my lord. Not at this time— at least, not one that any of the other members of the council would understand. But I have received a kind of . . . message."

"An augury?" Han-Zi leaned forward. "Some ill omen, then. If so, you know you may speak freely—it is your very job to report such things, and for us to abide by them if necessary."

"Yes . . . no . . . not exactly, but something of that nature." It was not in him to lie outright. Sai-Jun cursed his own need for honesty.

"Speak clearly, Sai-Jun."

"I cannot, my lord." Sai-Jun sighed in defeat. "But I ask you—I *beg* of you—to listen to me regardless. If not as your spiritual advisor, then as a friend asking for an extremely important favor. Please." He met Han-Zi's stare and held it, hoping his conviction would be enough to sway his lord's decision.

He waited, the room seeming to reverberate the heavy silence, as Han-Zi considered his words.

"Unless," Han-Zi replied finally, his words carefully considered, "you offer me good reason, it cannot be done. Not because I do not believe you, but because the other members of the council must believe *me*. I cannot delay such a meeting simply on a whim. It would be neither proper nor respectful. You know this."

"Then you must lie, my lord!"

"And say what?"

"Anything! Say your son is sick, say you yourself have been struck by illness, say you've had a vision from the gods—anything!"

"Sai-Jun . . ."

"Have I yet steered you wrong, my lord? Have I ever before acted inappropriately?" When no answer immediately came, Sai-Jun pressed what little advantage he had, throwing aside all thought of dignity and bowing so low that his forehead touched the ground, his palms flattened in front of him. He heard Han-Zi's low gasp at this—not even the lowest of the palace servants needed to demonstrate such obsequiousness in the course of their usual duties. "Please," he implored again, not even attempting to keep the sense of urgency he felt from his voice. "I am begging you, as I have never begged anything of you before now."

He held his breath and waited. And waited some more.

A heavy sigh. Cautiously, Sai-Jun raised his head slightly from the floor, his eyes finally meeting those of his lord's once more.

"Oh, get up. You know I cannot abide such courtly dramatics, just as I cannot refuse you now," Han-Zi said, exasperation coloring his voice. "You'll have your precious time."

"My lord?" Sai-Jun dared to hope.

Han-Zi gave a tight smile. "I do not know why you have asked this of me, but I *do* expect a full accounting later—and not only to me. The rest of the council will be most curious to hear your explanation, when the time comes. Do you heed?"

"Yes, my lord!" Despite the barely voiced rebuke and the obvious warning, Sai-Jun felt a flood of relief.

Han-Zi dismissed his spiritual advisor with a wave of his hand. "Very well. I give you three days. Do not make me regret it."

CHAPTER SIX

"Boy! More wine."

Shen-Fei froze for a moment, willing himself not to cringe, knowing that any such sign of weakness would do nothing but fan the flames of his father's anger. Still, he did not dare refuse the request, for all it was unusual. The only time Shen-Fei could recall his father drinking more than a single cup to accompany a private meal at home was the evening following the funeral of his wife, the Lady Mei—Shen-Fei's mother. The general had buried his grief in his wine that night, drinking himself so senseless that not even the servants could rouse his slumped form—but never again after that.

Shen-Fei would not have questioned it, nor thought to criticize, had his father shown more outward sign of his sorrow, no matter how many years later—but tonight, Shen-Ya's mood was clearly not one of sadness. In a foul mood even before the message had come from the bonded palace servants that the council, which was supposed to have been held tonight, had been delayed for three days, the general's temper was now one of clear belligerence.

He picked up his goblet and held it out, and despite his care, Shen-Fei's hands shook as he poured, splashing a few drops.

Shen-Ya gave his son a withering glare. "Clean that up. As if your clumsiness with the sword was not enough!"

Shen-Fei hurried to do as he was bid, nodding respectfully to show he was listening as his father spoke again.

"There was no excuse for such a delay! Listen to this, boy—

yes, *this* ridiculous message is what they sent me, and presumably every other member of the council." He began reciting from the parchment, squinting a little to make out the words against the flickering candlelight. "In light of a recent decision granted by our esteemed Lord Han-Zi, the council is hereby delayed until three days hence, where you shall present yourself as accustomed."

"Yes, Father."

"But it's what comes next that's even more ridiculous!" *This*, it appeared, was the way in which the message had been concluded. Alongside Lord Han-Zi's insignia was another, this somewhat smaller and less grand, but still notable for its presence. "There, right below my lord's. *Spiritual Advisor Sai-Jun*. Mark my words, *he* has something to do with this—after all, it does not say Lord Han-Zi made the decision, only that he granted it—and no doubt that conniving man used some crafty trick or other, or perhaps his honeyed words, to somehow convince Lord Han-Zi to agree to this . . . this . . . blatant power ploy!"

"Yes, Father."

Shen-Ya continued on in this vein for some time, his words growing progressively more foul-mouthed, as Shen-Fei nodded woodenly. Finally, realizing his father was far drunker than he'd assumed, Shen-Fei got slowly to his feet, murmuring an excuse, hoping to escape the ugly torrent of abuse.

Before he could reach the carved doorway, a vase shattered, scant inches above his head. The pieces fell about his feet—Shen-Ya's drunkenness had apparently not impaired his aim in the slightest.

"Did I give you permission to go?"

Shen-Fei caught his breath and turned, his gaze lowered. He bowed, hoping to appease. "No, Father."

Now red-faced with both rage and drink, Shen-Ya could barely get the words out. "Clean that mess up—that's right, boy, not a servant—*you!* Perhaps it will serve as a lesson to mind your manners and obey your elders. Even your poor mother would have been ashamed."

Shen-Fei's shoulders stiffened.

Oblivious, Shen-Ya continued his tirade, his tongue loosened enough that he spoke more to his son now in this moment, beyond sharp reprimands, than Shen-Fei could remember since he had been a child.

"What past sin did I commit to be *blessed* with a son so incompetent? Even the smallest task I give, you manage to bungle, from the home to the palace! I'm becoming a laughingstock among my own army. The general's own son—a milksop and an inept weakling who would rather scribble than take up arms."

Shen-Fei forced himself to carry on with his task, bending down to pick up the scattered remains of the vase—attempting to tune out the hurtful words by reminding himself, over and over, that his father could not truly mean them.

" . . . Barely even worth my time, much less my respect! For what did I spend hours and hours, training an apparent scribe when you should have been born a warrior . . ."

Don't listen, don't listen, he is drunk, he does not truly mean it . . .

" . . . As if I ask anything truly difficult? Yet your softness gets in the way, every gods-be-damned time! You certainly didn't get that from *my* bloodline—nay, it's your mother to blame for that . . ."

He doesn't mean it, he cannot, he's barely aware of what he's saying . . .

" . . . Has it made even the slightest difference? No matter how I push and cajole, you fail time and time again to deliver satisfactory results. My only child? Ha! *Her* only child. You were always hers, no matter how much I tried to instill the proper skills, the proper decorum in you when you were still young enough to learn. And now it may well be too late! It's as well she died and let me take over raising you — gods know I have struggled to undo the damage she was clearly responsible for . . ."

Don't listen, don't listen, it's the drink talking, he loved her just as much as I did, he must *have loved her . . .*

But Shen-Fei's hand involuntarily clenched, and the shard he was holding as he continued picking up the polished red lacquerware dug cruelly into his palm. A razor-thin line of blood began to seep from the cut.

"You accept a useless woman, you receive a useless boy. Yes, there's only her to blame for how you turned out —"

"Stop it!"

There was a ringing silence. Shen-Fei hardly knew he had spoken, but now that he had, he could not take it back. His hand continued to squeeze, causing the blood to run down his palm and over his wrist.

"What did you say to me?"

His father appeared more shocked than angry.

Despite himself, an almost hysterical smile crept over Shen-Fei's face. He could feel it twisting his expression, making him feel different than usual. For a brief moment, powerful.

"I said, stop it." His head spun. Was this what it was like to finally take a stand? To speak, for however brief a time, the words that had been building up in him over weeks, months, years?

Shen-Ya leaned forward, his hooded dark eyes reflecting disbelief and a renewed surge of dangerous anger, but Shen-Fei did not step back. It was too late to retreat now — he might as well carry on. And carry on he did, speaking words he never even knew he could think, let alone utter aloud.

"If you ever say that about Mother again, I'll sneak into your room at night. Maybe even tonight. When you're busy snoring away your drink, I will come to you, holding one of your own precious swords in *my* hand. You are no general of

45

mine. I don't have to be a warrior to best you. One stab in the right area. That's all it would take to prove it. Did you know that? Did you know *I* knew that?"

His father, still gaping throughout all of this, found his voice at last. "You'll do no such thing," he said dismissively, though his tone was uncharacteristically uncertain.

"Won't I, Father? Are you sure?" Seizing on his father's unease, Shen-Fei continued on, feeling a surge of panic-stricken laughter bubbling up inside him, eager to press his advantage with something he knew would strike home. He knew he probably looked insane. He *felt* almost insane. Why not let his father think so? "And then, *if* you're still alive, I will go to Spiritual Advisor Sai-Jun, and I will tell him what you've been up to. I will tell him *everything*."

There was another silence, so heavy it was almost a physical presence in the air.

Very slowly, Shen-Ya stood, walking with surprising softness toward his son. He stopped in front of Shen-Fei, looking him in the eye and leaning in close. Almost, Shen-Fei thought his father was about to embrace him or ruffle his hair — some gesture of long-forgotten paternal affection.

Then he raised his arm and struck.

Unable to duck in time, Shen-Fei was sent staggering by the force of the blow, a curious ringing in his ears as he fell back into the wall. Now he had nowhere to run as his father towered over him, inconsolable.

Shen-Ya was screaming, almost sobbing, as he rained down blow after blow, his face so twisted in rage it was all but unrecognizable. Shen-Fei could barely make out the torrent of words that swept over him. Like a raging storm, they threatened to overwhelm him as his father railed, now far beyond hearing anything more that Shen-Fei might have to say, no matter how crazed.

" . . . Knew you were weak the moment you emerged,

bawling, from that bitch's womb, the worthless runt who now cowers in front of me—the shame, the embarrassment of calling you my son—coward, weakling, fool, half-wit—!"

Shen-Fei bit his lip in an effort to remain silent as he was beaten without respite with both fists and feet, the spittle flying from his father's mouth along with his words. On and on it went, and his quiet seemed only to serve to enrage Shen-Ya further until, finally, several long minutes later, he stopped. Sweating, his robes rumpled, his face beet-red and breathing harshly, Shen-Ya spat at his son's slumped form and left the room without another word, his footsteps fading away in the distance. Even then, Shen-Fei did not dare move.

He didn't know how long he crouched there, waiting for something else to happen—for his father to return, for a servant to come, anything—but when he finally moved to get up, Shen-Fei saw the floor beneath him smeared with blood. His clothing was torn, and when he fingered his face, he knew there would be no way to explain away the bruises. It hurt to breathe—his ribs, he realized, might well be broken.

The silence of the house seemed deafening after what had just occurred. His ears still rung from his father's uncontrolled shrieks.

"Young master!" The voice made him jump. One of the house servants, a young kitchen maid, stood in the doorway, dismay and fear warring on her face. "Let me help you—" She began to scurry over.

"No . . . don't." Shen-Fei stopped her, fearing her kindness would only bring trouble for her. "You shouldn't touch . . . just let me . . ." Slowly, painfully, he worked his way to his feet, biting back a groan of agony.

From there, under the stares of the aghast servants, he shuffled to his own chambers, where it took an age for him to put a clean over-robe atop his torn and bloody clothing. Then he left, his feet taking over thought, guiding him to the one place where, against all logic, he felt he might find refuge — for whatever he did, he knew he could not remain where he was. Not another night would he willingly spend in his father's house — not for anyone or anything.

His steps were small and slow, and he barely managed to walk a straight path — but either minutes or hours later, he did not know which, he was finally stumbling through the halls of the palace, the guards staring but allowing the general's son to pass.

Eventually, comforted by the fact that his father would never think to venture down into the lower parts of the palace — now least of all given Shen-Fei's earlier words — the young man leaned against a wall and closed his eyes. Come the morning, he thought dazedly to himself, he would work out what to do.

Exhausted and pained beyond further thought, he slept.

CHAPTER SEVEN

Sai-Jun glanced up from where he had been flicking through the pages of some forgotten book in the palace library, unable to concentrate and reading the same words over and over again while taking none of them in.

He frowned, annoyed at first at the sound of running footsteps—hardly suitable for the palace corridors, let alone the library—but his annoyance was abruptly forgotten as Feng burst through the heavy doors and all but skidded to a stop in front of him, breathing heavily, his hair and robes disheveled.

"Sir—I—I've come directly from—"

"All right. Catch your breath," Sai-Jun said, and glanced quickly around. They were alone. He fought to control his impatience as Feng recovered, knowing his servant would tell him all as soon as he was able. "Speak," he finally bade when he saw that Feng had regained some of his composure.

"My lord, I was keeping watch as you told me. All appeared quiet until—well, there was screaming, sir."

"Screaming? From whom?" Sai-Jun demanded.

"Sir, I cannot be sure, as all of the occupants were within. But it was a man's voice—not screaming in pain, you understand, sir, but in anger. It continued for some minutes, then silence again."

"And then? What of the general?"

"He was still inside the home when I left, sir."

"And . . . his son? What of Shen-Fei?"

"Gone, sir. I saw him slip away, moving in the direction of

the palace, but I could not follow for fear of being seen . . . you bade me be discreet, sir." Feng winced slightly when Sai-Jun glared at him. "By the time I was able to leave without fear of being noticed, he had disappeared. I thought it best to find you immediately rather than search in vain. Sir, it may be that he is already somewhere nearby, perhaps even in the palace as we speak . . ."

Reminding himself the man had simply been following his orders as best as he could, Sai-Jun breathed heavily out of his nose, then nodded decisively. "You've done well," he said, much to Feng's clear relief. "Now, it's imperative that we find Shen-Fei as soon as possible. You're right, it's likely he's somewhere here in the palace already, for I do not know where else he might safely go at such a time. Fetch a lantern. We will search for him together. I don't want this to become public knowledge."

As Feng raced off to do his master's bidding, Sai-Jun stood for a long moment, his eyes closed. Despite his sense of urgency that bordered on panic, he made himself breathe slowly, deeply, focusing his attention inward. If ever there was a time for his abilities to manifest themselves, it was now.

At first, there was nothing but irritating darkness — nothing with which to guide him in any direction. He breathed in more deeply, then back out, forcing himself to patience. And then, after a long moment . . . *there*. A flicker. Something pulling at him, like the gentle tugging of a string. It was no more than the smallest of movements, but it was present, nonetheless.

"Sir."

He opened his eyes to see Feng staring at him. "Good. Let us go."

Feng held the lantern and followed as Sai-Jun led them steadily out of the library and into the maze of halls and corridors, each leading to different parts of the palace, from the apartments of various advisors and noblemen to the servant quarters. At a crossroads, Sai-Jun hesitated only briefly, then continued until they were climbing down an older set of stairs, these rarely used.

This part of the palace was quieter, dimmer, the rooms here far older. Different parts of the palace had seen successive renovations over the course of multiple generations of lords, and what had long ago been guest chambers for visiting dignitaries were now used mainly for storage. Soon enough there were no more torches lighting their path at all, and as they continued to the lowest parts of the palace, Feng had to hold the lantern high so they could progress safely through the darkness.

"Is anyone down here?" Sai-Jun's voice echoed from the walls bare of tapestries and down the pitch-black halls, then came back to meet him, sounding faint and ghostly. *Anyone down here . . .down here . . .*

But there was no answer, even as they peered into chambers filled with disused furniture, some covered with sheets to keep off the dust, others simply left to gradual ruin.

"Hello?"

Still nothing, and now they were nearing the end of this section of the palace and would soon be forced to turn around and go back the way they had come. Next to him, Feng shivered — it was certainly far cooler down here, where the underground levels of the palace saw no sunlight.

Sai-Jun sighed. He could discern no movement other than their own, neither physical nor with his inner senses. "Perhaps I was wrong . . ."

"Sir!" He looked at Feng sharply, and the servant held a finger to his lips. "I thought I heard . . ." he began to whisper, and both men abruptly turned at the sound of something else. It was barely there — little more than a slight shuffling that could easily have been some lost animal, a mouse or a shrew, but Sai-Jun turned swiftly to follow the sound.

"Shen-Fei?"

Somewhere on the edge of his vision, a shadow moved where it should not have. Sai-Jun rounded the corner . . . and there he was, slumped against a wall, his eyes closed and his hair loose and falling in tangles about his face. Even so, Sai-Jun knew him instantly.

"Shen-Fei!"

The young man gave a gasp, sounding afraid, and opened his eyes very slowly, as if even this small movement cost him great effort. "Don't . . ."

"Shen-Fei, it's me . . . it's Sai-Jun. Come, we need to get you out of here."

Shen-Fei gave another gasp, attempting to scramble to his feet of his own will. "No! I won't go back . . . please, I can't go back there . . ."

"You're not going back home, I promise you that. Come, take my arm."

"Promise . . . please, he'll kill me . . . or I'll kill him. I will!"

Sai-Jun did not stop to question this statement. He didn't know what Shen-Fei had been through this night, but he had no doubt it was extreme enough to make Shen-Fei say things he otherwise would not have.

"I swear by the gods, I will not take you back there," was all Sai-Jun said to this. Then he clasped Shen-Fei's hand, sealing his oath, and hauled him up by the arm.

Shen-Fei gave a hoarse scream, staggering and slumping over, and Sai-Jun had no choice then but to support the young man's body fully. He swore, more in unaccustomed panic than anything else, and Feng rushed to hold Shen-Fei's other side. Together, they manhandled the awkward weight back through the halls and up the stairs again.

When they finally reached the upper levels of the palace once more, all of them panting, Sai-Jun bade Feng stop. "I have him now. Go quickly to the Master Healer. Not any of his servants, you understand? Him alone. Tell him this needs to be kept secret, but tell him truthfully what you've witnessed here and that we require his services. Have him meet me in my private chambers as soon as possible. Tell him I will be in his debt."

Feng nodded and left at a smart pace, Sai-Jun walking more slowly behind him and then veering to the right toward his apartments. Looking now at Shen-Fei's alarmingly pale face and, from what Sai-Jun glimpsed beneath the over-robe, his blood-splattered clothes, there was little time to lose.

"Well?" Sai-Jun stopped from where he had been restlessly pacing as Master Healer Rai-Yu stood from where he had been kneeling by the sleeping platform.

"He'll live. No internal injuries." Like Sai-Jun, the Master Healer was a surprisingly young man, unmarried and only a few years Sai-Jun's senior. Having completed his inspection and gently sponged the dried blood from Shen-Fei's face and hands, he now washed his own hands in a separate basin of water, plain silver and unadorned save for his blue crest of office carved into the metal.

"And? What do you make of these?"

With Shen-Fei's arms bare, the sleeves of his under-robe pushed up, what had once been hidden, likely for years, was now clear: a network of what would have looked like scars had they been silvery-white, but were instead ink-black, criss-crossing their way from his wrists nearly to his elbows.

Sai-Jun had never seen the likes of them before, but his blood ran cold when he tried to imagine how exactly they had come to be there. It was clear to him, now, why Shen-Fei always insisted on wearing such cumbersomely heavy and formal clothing. Whoever or whatever had done this, it was clearly something he did not wish the world to know of.

"If they are wounds, they're not new," Rai-Yu pointed out,

his voice free of judgment. "Nor are they raised—no build-up of healing tissue around them. This is . . . most unusual."

"Magic?" Sai-Jun wondered aloud.

"Perhaps. You would know better than I of such things, Spiritual Advisor."

Sai-Jun frowned, unable to give this puzzle the thought it would need just now. There were yet more pressing matters. "What of the rest of his injuries?"

"Mostly deep bruising, along with several more superficial cuts. The most serious of his injuries are his ribs. Fortunately, none appear to be broken, but it will be some time before he is able to move around freely without pain. This was a beating, pure and simple."

Glancing at him, Sai-Jun saw that Rai-Yu's face was carefully blank, although the fact that he had come at Sai-Jun's request suggested he was on the spiritual advisor's side—or at least, was not his enemy. Council politics be damned—Sai-Jun would need to take this chance.

"His father did this." And though he forced his own expression to be calm as well, Sai-Jun's hands clenched of their own accord, and his voice was dark with an anger he could not conceal.

"Yes, I suspected as much. There are no marks here to suggest the young man fought back. And this would seem to be all his blood, no one else's." Rai-Yu continued to work, his hands steady as he began to bind Shen-Fei's ribs tightly with bandages. Once this was done, the master healer turned to prepare a draught. He had it ready in the space of a few minutes, all the ingredients seemingly prepared ahead of time. Feng had plainly told Rai-Yu all he had needed to know to effectively treat his unexpected patient.

"When he wakes, have him take this. He must drink all of it—it will help him sleep more peacefully and prevent fever. Do you intend to stay with him?"

"Of course I do," Sai-Jun all but snapped, and Rai-Yu raised an eyebrow.

"You seem rather close," he said bluntly. "It's unlike you, Spiritual Advisor."

Sai-Jun scowled further. "You don't think he's in need of protection?"

"I think it's unusual of you to offer it." Rai-Yu remained unperturbed. "But yes, companionship will be good for him. He could be startled into a panic if he wakes up alone. He may not even remember how he came to be here at all."

"I'll wait, then. However long it takes."

"Very well." The master healer prepared to take his leave. "It grows late. I will return tomorrow to see how he fares."

"Wait." Sai-Jun grabbed him by the wrist. "Don't tell anyone. Please."

Rai-Yu said nothing, merely looked at him, and Sai-Jun sighed. He had no right to order anything of Rai-Yu — they were of equal rank, and the master healer was Sai-Jun's senior.

"I know I have nothing to offer you at this moment but my thanks. But if there ever comes a time when you are in need of *my* help . . ."

Rai-Yu's sudden smile was kind — far kinder, Sai-Jun knew, than he could have expected. Councilmembers and noblemen traded in so-called favors all the time, and Rai-Yu might have offered a steep price that Sai-Jun would have had little option but to accept.

"Spiritual Advisor, I have seen nothing untoward. At least, not officially. Call this naught but a friendly evening call between colleagues if you will. We younger members of the council are few, after all, and must forge our own path in such times."

The relief Sai-Jun felt at this was outweighed only by a rush of gratitude. "Thank you." He had never meant those words more deeply.

Rai-Yu bowed — not formally, but as one friendly acquaintance might to another — and left, sliding the door softly closed behind him.

Letting out a breath, Sai-Jun pulled a floor cushion closer and kneeled at the side of the bed — his bed — careful not to disturb the still-unconscious Shen-Fei.

In that moment, even with his emotions in turmoil and his mind now turning to attempt to make sense of what he had seen this night, he knew he would do anything it took to keep Shen-Fei safe. Anything at all.

CHAPTER EIGHT

When Shen-Fei next became aware of his surroundings, it was to realize he was not leaning against a cold stone wall as he'd imagined, but lying on something soft. Dimly, he understood he must be stripped to his under-robes to be able to feel the slight pressure of smooth sheets against thinly clad skin.

The next thing he was aware of was a regular *thump, thump, thump* . . . it took a few moments to conclude it was the sound of his own heartbeat. His surroundings must be very quiet, then. He didn't want to open his eyes, lest he wake and find such soothing quiet to be only a dream.

Then he noticed the breathing. It too was quiet, peaceful, and his first thought was that it must likewise be his own. But when he breathed out, his ears told him that another breath drew in at the same time, so that another person must be very close to his ear. And this thought so surprised him that he couldn't help but snap his eyes open, stifling a groan when a flood of light assaulted his vision.

It was so bright that for a moment, all he could see was shifting flecks of white and gray, and hazy outlines of things from further across the room. He must have made a sound despite himself, because there came a slight movement beside him, and a face suddenly swam into vision. Dark eyes in a pale, narrow face, framed by hair that looked oddly mussed.

Sai-Jun.

Shen-Fei gaped.

They stared at each other for a moment, the spiritual

advisor looking almost as startled as Shen-Fei felt, before placing a hand on his forehead. "You're awake."

"Um . . . yes?" It wasn't like Sai-Jun to waste words or bother stating the obvious.

"Well. It's certainly about time."

That was more like it. For lack of anything else to say, Shen-Fei glanced around awkwardly and pulled the sheet up a little higher, covering his white under-robe, feeling exposed. "I . . . how long was I asleep?"

Sai-Jun looked out the window, and Shen-Fei followed his gaze. Judging by the shadows, the sun had evidently risen only an hour or so ago. "Two days. You don't remember?"

Shen-Fei shook his head, eyes wide. "Remember what?"

"You had a fever and did not wake, even when we tried to rouse you. The master healer himself was unable to make you drink the medicine he brewed for you. I — *we* — did not know if you would . . ." Sai-Jun cleared his throat. "Rai-Yu was quite worried for your wellbeing."

There was a pause, and Shen-Fei wondered if Sai-Jun knew how he sounded for a moment. Like he genuinely cared. Then it hit him.

"Two *days*?" He shot up, then muffled a cry of pain at the movement. It felt as though nearly all the bones and muscles in his chest sang out in discordant protest.

Sai-Jun pushed him gently back down. "I would not recommend doing that again."

"But . . . two days . . . gods, what must people — my father . . ."

"Peace." Sai-Jun held up a hand. "All appropriate messages have been sent. Officially, you've simply been ill. As the general's son, we naturally ensured you would receive the best of care here in the palace. However, as yet, nobody knows this but I, the master healer, and now your father. He has not been here . . . and if he did happen to show his face, I would be sure to show him something in return."

He turned away briefly, his face hidden, and Shen-Fei wondered at the way Sai-Jun's voice had seemed to tremble slightly.

Shen-Fei lay still awhile, thinking. The quiet chatter of bird song outside was peaceful, completely at odds with the violence that had been wrought in his father's house. After a few more moments had passed, he finally glanced back over at Sai-Jun, knowing there was no way the spiritual advisor had not seen.

"You know, don't you?"

"Know what?"

Shen-Fei smiled a little bitterly. "Since when have you been one to play games?"

Sai-Jun let out an explosive sigh. "Fine. I assume you refer to the markings on your arms—in which case, yes, I am aware. The master healer and I both witnessed them as we were caring for you."

"And?"

"And what? What is it you would have me say?" Shen-Fei gaped anew as Sai-Jun stood, pacing the room as though unable to contain his frustration. "Were you going to go your entire life hiding it? For whom? For *what*? Is this why you pushed me away? Why you refused to let me so much as touch—" He broke off with an impatient shake of his head, plainly upset.

Shen-Fei had never seen Sai-Jun so rattled. He had hardly guessed Sai-Jun had such emotions to begin with. "No . . . well, I suppose . . . but who cares? What does it matter now?"

"What does it *matter*?" Sai-Jun stared at him. "Are you truly that foolish? Don't you know I . . . how can you not have seen . . ."

Shen-Fei glared. "It seemed to me," he said steadily, "that you were just as eager as I, if not more so, for me to leave that night."

"Then you're a prize idiot!" Sai-Jun rounded on him, glaring fiercely.

"And you're ten times worse! What was I supposed to think? You hide your feelings so well, I hardly knew you had any! I left because I was afraid *these* were all you would see from then on, if you would deign to look upon me at all, knowing what I hid . . ." He held out his scarred arms in disgust, the lines crisscrossing upward, as dark and obvious as ink staining what should have been clean parchment. Angrily, he yanked the sleeves of his white under-robe back down to cover his wrists. "And you? What's *your* excuse?" he burst out next. "What is the great spiritual advisor so afraid of?"

Sai-Jun scowled, looking everywhere but at Shen-Fei, then let out another sigh, a little softer this time. "You," he admitted finally, still gazing determinedly out of the window. "I was hurt—and yes, afraid—that the only person I'd ever dared care about, and the only one who'd ever shown an interest in me—not my aspirations, not my abilities as one marked by the gods, but *me*—had rejected me after a single night." His eyes finally turned to Shen-Fei, still glaring. "There. Is that what you so wished to hear?"

Shen-Fei reached out an arm, then thought better of it. "And now?" he asked quietly. "Now that you know . . . now that you've seen these . . . my own *marks* for yourself . . ." Self-loathing, not only for those same markings, but for what he had become and all he had allowed himself to endure over the years, welled up.

But Sai-Jun gripped his wrist before Shen-Fei could fully hide his arms back under the bedcovers. "I don't care," he whispered fiercely. "Did you truly think I would? *I*?"

"I don't know." Shen-Fei shook his head, feeling the tears well up. "Nobody has seen these. *Nobody*, except . . ." He swallowed and tried again. "And it's not just because I find them so repulsive. It's . . . years ago, when he . . . when my father . . ." He shook his head again and closed his eyes. The secret was out now. What did it matter what else Sai-Jun knew? A single, traitorous tear squeezed its way out and slid slowly down his cheek.

"Don't."

"Don't what?" Shen-Fei sniffed.

"Don't hide. Not from me. Not anymore. Please?"

"The great spiritual advisor Sai-Jun, actually begging for something?" Shen-Fei tried to smile, to inject some sarcasm into his voice, but he knew all he sounded was broken.

"You might be surprised how much of that I seem to have been doing of late."

Shen-Fei's eyes opened in surprise as he felt the touch of a finger stopping the tear in its tracks and wiping it carefully away. "I never knew you cared so much," he spoke again, this time in wonder, before he could stop himself.

"You'd be surprised," Sai-Jun murmured again, and the edges of his mouth curved up in a smile so unexpectedly sweet that for the life of him, Shen-Fei could only continue to stare.

For a while after that, time passed blissfully slowly. Master Healer Rai-Yu came and went again, declaring himself satisfied, and to Shen-Fei's immense relief, asking no questions other than how his patient was feeling.

After this, Sai-Jun brought food and drink, and they sat together, eating slowly, while it finally dawned on Shen-Fei that despite the utilitarian furnishings, the lack of rich decoration, this was the spiritual advisor's private apartments—that he was lying in Sai-Jun's own *bed*—and that Sai-Jun not only didn't seem to mind, but seemed to be actively doing his best to make Shen-Fei stay there.

They spoke of small things for a while, inconsequential things that gradually helped to put Shen-Fei's mind at ease and made him see that beneath Sai-Jun's usually cold exterior lay a heart of his own that was as easily bruised as any other. Sai-Jun spoke openly, albeit somewhat haltingly, of his childhood, his bewilderment and wonder at being taken at a young age from a small farming village to the palace to study when his powers had become apparent. Of the parents who had raised him, not wealthy, but always ready with a kind word or piece of practical advice.

In return, Shen-Fei spoke of his love of art and drawing, and how his mother, the Lady Mei, had bid him continue, to show her the finely inked sketches of both real animals and whimsical creatures he had created as a child when he was meant to be paying attention to his lessons. Of her own love of brewing tea, when she had still been strong enough to sit awhile and receive guests — and then, when this had no longer been possible, her enjoyment of music, which she could listen to for hours on end as she lay in bed and stared out at her small garden, bedecked with colorful blossoms and a small pond that, on days with clear skies, reflected the water up onto the eaves.

Shen-Fei's childhood seemed long past now, as Sai-Jun's no doubt seemed to him. He wished they had talked of such things far sooner, back when things had been simpler and they had not wasted months, years of longing, on bitterness caused by silence and misunderstandings. The nostalgia in Sai-Jun's voice, the wry quirk of his mouth as he remembered times gone by, made Shen-Fei realize all over again that there was far more to the man than he presented to the outside world — and why Shen-Fei had fallen in love with such a seemingly cold and detached person to begin with. Under the surface lay a wealth of emotion, of capacity to love, and it made Shen-Fei want things that he had long since convinced himself would never come to fruition.

Finally, the conversation shifted onto more important matters, as Shen-Fei knew it must. Sai-Jun shifted, a more serious expression coming over his face as he straightened his back from where he still kneeled attentively on a plain black cushion beside the sleeping platform.

"You know the council is planned for tomorrow night," he said carefully, looking at Shen-Fei as if to make sure he wouldn't suddenly fly into a panic. "If possible, I wish you to accompany me."

Shen-Fei stared, wondering if the spiritual advisor had suddenly taken leave of his senses. "I don't belong at council! And just what do you think my father would do if he knew that you and I — that he knew I had told you — "

Sai-Jun interrupted his protests. "I know. And this is partially what I'm counting on. Shen-Fei, I have a plan, but I need your cooperation to see it through. Will you help? Please? You know I would not ask if there was any other way."

"I don't know." Shen-Fei looked away. "What will happen . . . to my father? Are you going to kill him?" he asked in sudden dread.

"No. But I don't know what will become of him after. It depends."

"On what?"

"Well . . . on you. But I need to know something first."

"What?" Shen-Fei had an uneasy feeling he already knew.

"The truth about this." He held up Shen-Fei's arms, his touch achingly gentle. "I need to know how this came to pass, and why."

"I . . . I can't tell you," Shen-Fei replied miserably.

"Why not? The guilt does not lie with you, surely you must know this."

"He's my father!" Shen-Fei burst out. "I hate him for what he's done, for everything that's happened! I *hate* him!" He bit

63

his lip. "But he's the only family I have left. And even if he were not, as his son, I must lawfully obey . . ."

"Shen-Fei, he *must* account for what he's done. Will you let him get away with it? Will you allow his abuse of you to continue? And what if he does the same to another? Would you have that on your conscience, knowing you might have prevented such a thing from occurring?"

Wordlessly, Shen-Fei shook his head. He knew what Sai-Jun said was the truth, nothing more and nothing less, but for all his hatred, he did not know if he could bring himself to stand before the council and say what no doubt needed to be said. He knew this was what Sai-Jun was getting at. But killing his father in cold blood — as he remembered, in the heat of his pain and his rage, that he had claimed he would do — would have seemed a better sentence than that. To someone like the general, public shame would be a fate worse than death.

"You are right about one thing," Sai-Jun continued, his voice heavy. "As your father, Shen-Ya still has a lawful claim on you, and always will, unless . . ."

And there it was. Sai-Jun had known exactly what Shen-Fei had long hesitated to do. "Unless I speak out against him and prove his crimes." But could he really do that? Could he truly betray his own flesh and blood, and the person who, despite all, had raised him to manhood?

"Yes."

There was a long silence, in which Shen-Fei could barely breathe, his heart hammered so painfully. Finally, he raised his eyes to meet those of the spiritual advisor's.

"I will tell you," he said. "Only promise me you won't kill him. Lord Han-Zi will do what he must, but it is not up to you. Allow the council to decide, even if their will is not in line with yours. Will you swear it?"

Sai-Jun dipped his head in acknowledgment. "I swear," he

said. "The gods as my witnesses, I will not take part in pronouncing sentence upon Shen-Ya."

"Then come closer."

Sai-Jun leaned forward, his ear close to Shen-Fei's mouth.

And finally, after years of silence, in a voice that was barely above a whisper, Shen-Fei told him everything.

CHAPTER NINE

"How are you feeling? Do you experience any stabbing pain when you lie still or breathe in deeply?"

"No." Shen-Fei shook his head as the master healer continued to prod delicately at his injuries, Sai-Jun watching carefully. His plan could only go ahead if Shen-Fei was present at council—and with Shen-Fei's blessing, Sai-Jun had already left for a time to collect what evidence he must for that—but nonetheless, Sai-Jun refused to sacrifice safety. This afternoon, he had asked Rai-Yu to check his patient over once more—much to Shen-Fei's protestations—to make sure he was well enough to attend. The meeting, Sai-Jun had warned, could and likely would go on for some time before their plan was put into action.

"How about elsewhere on your body? Do your other bruises pain you when left untouched?"

"Not really." Shen-Fei appeared awkward, seemingly unaccustomed to this kind of attention, and Sai-Jun smiled inwardly as the young man flushed a little, darting an entreating look back over at the spiritual advisor as if to ask, *When will this be over?*

"Good. I understand you will be joining us this evening, and you do seem to be doing well enough to do so," Rai-Yu continued. "I shall of course keep that little piece of information between us." Sai-Jun breathed a sigh of relief as Rai-Yu glanced over at him. "But I expect you'll create quite a stir. I do hope," he added a little more pointedly, "that Spiritual Advisor Sai-Jun will look after you properly, Shen-Fei. I don't know what you two have in mind, but I advise most strongly against any kind of strenuous activity. Yes?"

Sai-Jun broke in. "Rest assured, I have no intention of putting Shen-Fei in harm's way. With so many other witnesses present—guards included—I don't anticipate any physical danger."

"Very well, then." Rai-Yu smiled down at his patient. "Be sure to keep your ribs tightly bound like this for at least the next few days—it will ease the discomfort. Do not get them wet—remove them when you bathe and have Sai-Jun replace them afterward. Otherwise, you should be largely free to do as you like, so long as you exercise careful restraint. You know where to find me if needed."

Though not necessary, Sai-Jun bowed deeply as the master healer left the room, grateful beyond measure for his expertise.

"Well . . ." Shen-Fei was struggling to replace his overrobe, still a little red-faced. "That's good news."

"Indeed. Now, do not take this the wrong way, but . . ."

"What?"

Sai-Jun smiled. "You *are* in need of a bath."

Shen-Fei bent his head a little and sniffed. "I am, aren't I?" He seemed suddenly mortified. "Gods. I'm sorry, I didn't realize . . ."

"Don't apologize. It's not your fault. Come—I'll help with the rest of your clothes, then I'll take you somewhere special," he promised.

Steam rose gently from a network of connected pools—one of the two large bathing chambers in the palace, this one reserved only for the highest levels of advisors and their families. Some of the pools here were small and round, big enough only for one person to comfortably relax, while others were far larger, with space enough for several people to sit, lie, or even swim a little if they so desired.

"I've never been in here before," Shen-Fei commented, looking around with an expression of awe. "It's far bigger than I'd imagined."

"One of the perks of living in the palace," Sai-Jun admitted. "Though I keep my apartments sparse enough, or so I'm told, I like to come here often, especially during times when I know I'll likely be alone. Here, let me help you." Ignoring Shen-Fei's yelp of surprise, Sai-Jun quickly began undressing him, though still mindful of his bruised ribs and assortment of other bruises. Male nudity, when in a private setting, was common enough, but Shen-Fei clearly had more modesty than most, the way he was averting his gaze. Then Sai-Jun mentally kicked himself. Of course he did. He hadn't let any-one see him for years — not since his arms had been so scarred. No wonder he seemed almost constantly skittish. Instinc-tively, the young man probably still fought to hide himself away, ashamed and afraid of what would happen if he did not.

"It's all right." Sai-Jun met his gaze, wanting to make sure Shen-Fei understood. "If you don't want me to look at them, I won't. But understand this. Whether you like it or not, your marks are a part of you, and as such, they will never be a thing of ugliness to me. Know that I consider you as much marked by the gods as I."

Curse it, now *he* was blushing. Perhaps Shen-Fei had been right when they'd spoken of their feelings yesterday, accusing Sai-Jun of emotionlessness — even before he had taken on the role of spiritual advisor, he had closed himself off, seeking to build a barrier to protect against his own loneliness, and it felt odd to now allow himself to be so honest. So vulnerable.

When they both stood naked, Sai-Jun, not allowing his gaze to wander as he otherwise might have been tempted to do, led them to one of the larger pools, helping Shen-Fei to sit first before they slid gradually in.

"Ahh . . ." Shen-Fei sighed in relief. "This feels amazing."

"Good. I always feel the same." The hot water soothed aching and tensed muscles, and beside him, he saw Shen-Fei sink a little deeper, his eyes slipping closed.

"Truly, this is heavenly. Thank you for sharing this place with me."

"It's nothing." Sai-Jun felt awkward for a moment. Shen-Fei deserved to be happy. If Sai-Jun had his way, this was the very least he could do to make sure that happened. "Here. Sit up a little and lean your head against the wall, or on me if you'd rather. I'll wash your hair for you."

"Really?" Shen-Fei smiled shyly. "I've never . . . I mean, not since I was a young boy and my mother was still . . ." He trailed off, his smile fading.

"It's nothing," Sai-Jun murmured again.

Tucked into small alcoves here and there were precious colored bottles of glass, each containing liquid mixtures for washing the hair and body, and he took one of these bottles and allowed some of the liquid to trickle onto his hand. Shen-Fei groaned a little, clear appreciation in the sound, as Sai-Jun began to gently massage this into his scalp.

"That feels . . ."

"Good?"

"Better than good." He hummed again as Sai-Jun continued his ministrations, gradually working from the front to the back, then digging in a little more deeply with his fingers, purely to hear Shen-Fei moan again. "Oh, yes . . ." Sai-Jun chuckled a little, and Shen-Fei sighed. "Don't stop now."

"I hadn't planned on it."

Shen-Fei's eyes opened. He stared at Sai-Jun for a moment, and his tongue darted out to wet his mouth. Sai-Jun stared boldly back. He knew how it had sounded—and provided Shen-Fei wanted it too, the spiritual advisor had every intention of making up for lost time.

"Do . . . you really desire . . ."

"You?" Sai-Jun made sure Shen-Fei knew he was staring now. He would not lose this chance again—not because of his pride, or because he was too afraid to ask for what he wanted. He had learned his lesson. "Every last inch."

"Gods . . ." Shen-Fei's face flamed, even his ears turning a bright red. "I never thought I'd hear you of all people . . ."

"Only if you want it too," Sai-Jun hastened to say, partly to stop himself from blushing just as fiercely, but mostly because he didn't want to push too hard or scare Shen-Fei away. He'd made his desire blatant enough—now he needed to know Shen-Fei wanted him in return. If not, he knew he'd be disappointed—bitterly so—but that wouldn't change the way he felt. He regretted none of the actions he'd taken these past three days. Nor would he ever.

"I do. But . . ."

"Not now?"

"No, now's good," Shen-Fei said hastily. "Believe me. It's just . . . *here*? In the bathing chamber? What if someone walks in?"

"They won't," Sai-Jun assured him. "I promise."

"How do you know?"

Sai-Jun barely suppressed a grin. "Because I took certain steps to ensure it. Any visitors will find the door to be stuck fast until I wish otherwise."

"You . . ." Shen-Fei splashed him playfully. "I can't believe you'd use your gifts for something so frivolous."

"Frivolous, you say? Never that. They are used only as necessary." Sai-Jun did grin now, and their laughter echoed around the chamber. "Here." Sai-Jun helped Shen-Fei back out of the bath, took a pitcher of water, and poured it over his hair. The suds bubbled to the ground, where cleverly placed drains took the soiled water safely away from the clean pool

Marked by the Gods

of water and underground.

Then Sai-Jun took up a cake of soap and, as Shen-Fei leaned against him for support, began sliding it over the young man's body. His skin was smooth, his muscles more pronounced than Sai-Jun's, and the spiritual advisor enjoyed watching the soap glide over them, following the natural dips and crevices of his form.

The action gradually turned more sensual, Shen-Fei gasping a little and turning so that their faces were closer together. Sai-Jun didn't need to look to see that Shen-Fei was deeply aroused—he could feel the energy like magic, humming softly about them in the air. He, too, was quickly becoming affected by it, his member stiffening and nudging against Shen-Fei's lower stomach.

Intentionally, Shen-Fei repositioned himself slightly so that their arousals touched, and Sai-Jun shivered a little. In the year between their only interlude, he had not touched another man or woman, nor allowed himself to be touched, and what he felt now was all the more intense for it.

Shen-Fei's breathing grew heavier, and his mouth fell slightly open as he panted. His eyes looked slightly glazed. "Sai-Jun . . . please . . ."

"Don't worry. I've got you."

"Oooh . . ." The young man squirmed in his grasp, the soap making their bodies slip against one another with wet, squelching sounds, the movement less controlled and more frantic now.

Taking the hint, Sai-Jun grasped Shen-Fei's member in his hand. It too was slick and slippery, leaking fluid mixing with water and sweat, the steam from their surroundings overheating them both.

Shen-Fei buried his face in Sai-Jun's shoulder, his body trembling, his gasps raw and needy. He too, Sai-Jun remembered, had likely not experienced the touch of another in this way since their previous encounter a year since.

Determined to make this experience a pleasurable one for Shen-Fei, to put his needs first, Sai-Jun ignored his own aching desire for the moment and continued to stroke, slow at first, then gradually harder and faster as Shen-Fei's gasps grew in volume.

"Yes, *yes*, oh gods, if . . . I can't—I'm going to . . ."

A few final, purposeful jerks were all it took to tip Shen-Fei over the edge. The young man gave one last powerful shudder and cried out, the sound of his release echoing back at them from the walls.

Only then, as Shen-Fei half-sat, half-reclined against him, catching his breath, his body still shivering in the aftershocks of his climax, did Sai-Jun take his own arousal and bite his lip against a second resounding cry, his mind and body slipping into blissful relief as he allowed the proof of his desire to overtake him, his seed spilling shamelessly over his fingers and to the tiled ground.

CHAPTER TEN

"Ready?"

They stood together in front of the imposingly tall doors leading to the council chambers, their height only emphasized by the incongruous lack of any paint or carvings marking the dark, heavy wood.

Sai-Jun appeared as composed as he usually did, as though he was simply going about his duties like any other day.

"Y-yes." Shen-Fei heard the slight catch in his own voice and winced. Why could he never be as calm?

"Do not be afraid. You will remain by my side, and Lord Han-Zi is nothing if not just. He will listen and judge fairly. Come." With that, Sai-Jun knocked thrice, pushed open the doors, and strode in, looking every inch the confident spiritual advisor in his most formal of sweeping black robes, these edged in silver and embroidered at the back with the crest of his office, also in eye-catching silver. Shen-Fei scuttled after him in his borrowed house robes, feeling like an imposter in these grand chambers.

"Lord Han-Zi." Sai-Jun bowed before the dais where the lord of all Foshana kneeled on a large floor cushion, bold white embroidered with gold, Shen-Fei following suit.

The ruler of the province glanced at them, smiled briefly, then wiped his face clean of expression as was proper before nodding a formal greeting of his own. "Welcome, Spiritual Advisor Sai-Jun. Welcome, Shen-Fei, son of General Shen-Ya. You are both expected. Please." He gestured them to their seats, and Sai-Jun led them there, bowing and murmuring greetings to others he passed along the way. There was a slight stir, but if some looked surprised to see Shen-Fei there, they had heard Lord Han-Zi's remarks and dared say nothing publicly.

Shen-Fei was not personally acquainted with most of these men, although he had seen some in passing—the master of trade, the master treasurer, the head secretary. The general—Shen-Fei felt his heart beat yet faster at the thought of his father—was not yet in attendance. He caught the steady gaze of Master Healer Rai-Yu in his blue-edged formal robes, who acknowledged him with a small nod from across the room. At least he knew one other friendly face here.

His father was one of the last councilmen to enter the chamber. When Shen-Ya caught sight of his son, his eyes narrowed and his mouth worked furiously as though he wanted to say something, but he glanced around at everyone else already kneeling on their cushions and held himself in check. Sai-Jun affected not to notice when the general turned his glare on him, and Shen-Fei wondered again at the man's self-control. For his own part, his limbs were trembling beneath the heavy folds of his robes.

Finally, at Lord Han-Zi's nod, a guard moved to shut the large chamber doors, the windowless room now lit entirely by lamps. Lord Han-Zi stood, and the already quiet room fell completely silent. Then the ruler of Foshana spread his arms to indicate everyone gathered together.

"Greetings to you all. I thank you for coming, and for your patience in the face of this meeting's unexpected delay. I hereby declare commencement of the council!"

To Shen-Fei's surprise, relatively little of significance appeared to happen next. The measured talking, mostly from pre-prepared scrolls, seemed endless. Every now and again, voices became slightly raised in disagreement, but most men present simply acknowledged each speaker with nods of outward acceptance. The few guards and servants present remained silent in the background as each council member took their turn to stand and deliver what, to Shen-Fei at least, seemed to be the dullest of reports.

Glancing at Sai-Jun every now and then, the spiritual advisor looked to be listening intently to the proceedings, barely reacting to anything and speaking not at all. The other members of the council appeared equally as focused, although their emotions were sometimes a little more apparent — satisfaction, anger, or surprise flitted across their faces from time to time before their expressions were wiped conspicuously clean again.

Shen-Fei had expected something far more dramatic. "If this is what it's like to be a member of council, count me out," he muttered to Sai-Jun, who briefly looked like he was repressing a smile. He had not yet stood up to speak, and with every moment that passed, the tension in Shen-Fei grew, knowing what was still to come.

Finally, there came an expectant hush, and Shen-Fei realized all faces were now pointing in Sai-Jun's direction. His heart thumped loudly as the spiritual advisor stood, carefully rearranging his robes and looking around the room at each face before speaking, his bearing serene yet confident. He was one of the few who held no scroll, instead choosing to address his fellow council members directly.

"My lords," he began in quiet tones that nonetheless seemed to carry effortlessly around the room. "Before I begin my report, I have something else of import to discuss. I beg your forbearance to do so now."

At this, many of the other council members looked startled. Clearly, they had not expected any such deviation from the norm. The attentive atmosphere intensified, some members even leaning forward a little from where they knelt.

"I propose the immediate removal of General Shen-Ya from his position and from this council," Sai-Jun continued with nothing in the way of preface. His voice held no inflection, as though he were merely reporting on the time of day or the weather.

There was a profound silence before the room erupted, voices suddenly clamoring for attention. Many of the men present stood, gesturing sharply as they spoke. Sai-Jun waited, making no attempt to speak over the din, his posture erect and his hands still at his sides, showing neither alarm nor any other emotion until, slowly, the noise subsided.

For his part, Shen-Ya had said nothing up until now, but when the voices died down, he faced Sai-Jun with a look of such intense hatred that Shen-Fei inadvertently shuffled backward.

"What can you mean by this?" the general demanded. "My lords, this is madness! I suggest the spiritual advisor explain himself at once, or be ejected from council for making such a ludicrous proposition."

"Certainly I shall explain myself," Sai-Jun answered, not deigning to raise his own voice. "My lords, I have knowledge that General Shen-Ya has committed such crimes that will make his removal from council inevitable by the very laws of this province."

"How dare you accuse me of any such crime? Your words are baseless, your lies shameful! Lord Han-Zi, there is no crime I could have possibly — "

"It seems to me, my lord general" — the master healer broke in softly, making a pacifying gesture — "that we should at least hear the spiritual advisor out. Surely if he is mistaken, no harm will be done to you or your reputation."

"And what right have you to speak in defense of him, Master Healer? You know nothing of this, and I will not simply stand by as my name is besmirched, no matter how pretty his words!" Shen-Ya scowled, one hand clenching as though he yearned to grip a weapon. "Do *you* stand for this, my lords?" he entreated the men surrounding him.

There came a chorus of mutters in response, some council members clearly taking Shen-Ya's side, others looking merely bewildered at this turn of events. More men stood, gesturing sharply, and the volume of voices rose.

"Be silent and be seated!" Lord Han-Zi commanded. Shen-Ya snapped his mouth shut at this, as did everyone else in the room. "Spiritual Advisor Sai-Jun," the lord continued into the abrupt silence. "You have my permission to proceed, and all here shall listen respectfully. But make your account succinct and to the point, I pray you. There are some here whose patience is wearing thin."

"Yes, my lord. If I may?" Sai-Jun strode to the front of the room so that he stood closer to the dais, facing all other members of the council. "I have proof of the crimes of which I speak, these being the following. Theft. Misappropriation of palace items. And torture."

Another moment of resounding silence met these words, and this time, the general was the first to break it.

"What do you mean by this?" Shen-Ya was apoplectic with rage, his face now such a furious red it looked almost purple. His finger shook with barely repressed fury as he pointed at Sai-Jun. "You arrogant fool, your words are as unfounded as they are offensive! Where is this so-called proof?"

"The proof is currently seated before you, my lords."

Slowly, catching his meaning, all eyes were suddenly on Shen-Fei.

Taking his cue, as Sai-Jun had earlier instructed him to do, Shen-Fei got up and walked on shaking legs to stand beside the spiritual advisor. Then, bowing before the gathering but without saying a word, Shen-Fei held one arm high and drew back his sleeve to the elbow.

He wore no further layer of clothing underneath, and even in the relatively dim light, the black marks from the wrist upward stood out vividly like lines on a map. All other men present craned their heads, staring unabashedly.

"And what, pray tell, is this supposed to prove, exactly?" Shen-Ya's voice was defiant. "Whatever these . . . decorations on the boy's arm, I know nothing of them. How did they come to be there, and if indeed any person is responsible for them, then who? This is no proof—this is a trick, its motive borne from petty dislike. How you can even dare—"

"It is no trick," Sai-Jun interrupted. "My lord Han-Zi will know, sure enough, what such markings imply. They were not man-made, but created through magical means—a form of torture, indeed. Though this was outlawed in the final years of his father's reign, and all instruments of its kind ordered destroyed, you took it upon yourself to steal a certain item, did you not? And then, years later, you used this item on your own son. Is it not so, General Shen-Ya?"

"Enough." Lord Han-Zi stood, and Shen-Ya fell silent again. The ruler strode forward, inspecting the marks on Shen-Fei's arm for himself, touching them gently with his fingertips, his face devoid of emotion. Then he turned and retook his seat.

The chamber waited.

"It is so," Lord Han-Zi said finally into the ringing silence. "These marks were made with such an item as Spiritual Advisor Sai-Jun describes. How it found its way into another's hands, I do not know. But I should dearly like to find out." He leveled a glance at Shen-Ya, who was now opening and shutting his mouth, seemingly lost for words.

"It wasn't me!" he declared finally. "These filthy lies spouted by this so-called *advisor* are no less outrageous for their single element of truth! Again, I say, where is your proof that I was the one responsible? You are basing your words purely on your dislike for me, nothing more."

"Spiritual Advisor, that much is true," Lord Han-Zi spoke again. "If you wish to accuse General Shen-Ya of this crime, you must show proof that he personally was the one who committed it."

Shen-Ya's expression grew more confident. "Well?" he demanded. "If no such proof is forthcoming, I suggest we speak next of the consequences of *your* actions."

It was time. Shen-Fei looked his father square in the eye. "We have proof," he said quietly, willing his voice not to tremble at what he knew was about to take place.

"We will show you now." Sai-Jun made a sweeping gesture with his arm.

Without warning, the flicking lamps spaced around the room dimmed. Startled sounds followed, and Shen-Ya's voice sounded once more, anger mixed with alarm. Finally, the room fell quiet once again as all present stared at the vision beginning to unfold before them.

CHAPTER ELEVEN

The scene played out like a life-sized illustrated scroll, its pictures brought to life for all to witness.

Sai-Jun focused all of his energy into the age-old spell as the vision began to unfurl in front of him, blurred edges gradually coming together to form a more solid image. This was difficult to do—not only did the spell itself take a considerable amount of energy, but he badly wanted to steal a glance at Shen-Fei and make sure he was all right. What must it be like to re-live, this time as a bystander, something so terrible, knowing full well what was about to take place, and that others were watching and judging for themselves? Still, he persevered, knowing that the smallest distraction might cause the spell to cease and the vision to disappear—and without it, his accusation of Shen-Ya had no grounding. So Sai-Jun concentrated fiercely, hardly daring to blink, as the scene continued to progress, just as though he were watching something happen in real life.

First, an apparition of two figures—the first, an unmistakably younger version of Shen-Fei, still a boy on the cusp of manhood, standing before a second figure, his father. But for the general's somewhat thicker and darker hair, he looked much unchanged from his present self. The younger Shen-Fei was kneeling, his father standing imposingly before him. Both figures were dressed in stark white funeral robes, the red-crested decorations on the walls in the background making it evident that they were somewhere in their family home.

"Do not argue with me, boy, or you will regret it, I promise you," Shen-Ya hissed. "You will not sully the name of your mother in a time of mourning. Do not shame me by repeating such slander publicly!"

"Please, Father, listen to me! I fear she was poisoned— maybe by someone who has cause to be jealous of your position and influence. Such poison could easily have been meant for you—"

"Ridiculous! Your mother has always been fragile—gods know the woman was ill long before I married her. Her own family can attest to that."

"But she wasn't dying!" Shen-Fei argued, the pain plain on his face. "If you would just hear me and speak to the master healer, he might be able to conduct an examination—"

"Silence!" Shen-Ya commanded. "I will do no such thing! The idea of having her body violated by such means . . . it disgusts me! Will you not let your own mother rest in peace?"

"You *must* listen!" Shen-Fei begged. "Her death wasn't natural! She may never have been in good health, but she was well enough when I saw her last—I know it, we spoke for hours! She looked at my pictures, sat still as I drew her likeness . . ." He trailed off, quailing at his father's look of contempt.

"Then perhaps *you're* partially to blame! Tiring her out time and time again, making her pretend to show interest for the sake of your pride—and for what, I ask? *Pictures!*" Shen-Ya practically spat the word. "The general's own son, barely proficient with the sword, and he wastes his time cooped up who knows where, drawing! Is this what you've been up to whenever you're not in the training yard?"

Shen-Fei had turned pale. "I'm not to blame," he whispered. "She was well . . . she asked to see . . ."

"Get out!"

"Father, I–"

"*Get out!*"

Shen-Fei stood, about to obey. Then he squared his shoulders, his expression changing to one of grim determination. "No."

"Boy, do not try me—"

"Not until you hear me! I don't care what you say, Mother was *not* so seriously ill as to die so suddenly! And if you refuse to do anything about it, then . . . then I will!"

Shen-Ya was quiet for a moment. When he eventually spoke again, his voice was much lower. The threat in his voice was so clear that Sai-Jun, still focusing hard on maintaining the vision, felt his neck prickling with warning. "And what, exactly, do you mean by that?"

Despite his obvious misgivings, the younger Shen-Fei squared his shoulders again. "I'll send a message to the master healer myself, imploring him to examine Mother's body before it's burned tomorrow."

"Boy." Shen-Ya's voice emerged as a growl. "You'll do nothing of the sort."

"I will."

"You will not."

"I will!"

His shout rang out, and the two figures stood there a moment, glaring at one another other.

Then, Shen-Ya's figure abruptly left the vision. Shen-Fei stood up but remained in place, looking confused. "Father?" he called.

Nothing happened for several long moments. Sai-Jun heard mutters around him from the other council members. "Wait!" he instructed tersely, gritting his teeth, struggling to maintain the vision amid the interruption, and the room fell silent again.

Without warning, the vision of Shen-Ya re-entered the room, holding something tightly wrapped in dark cloth. Shen-Fei took an instinctive step back. "What's that?"

"Hold out your hands."

"What for?"

"Do it!"

"No . . ." His fear was apparent.

"Boy!" The pair tussled for a moment, but Shen-Ya's far superior strength easily got the best of his young son. He yanked Shen-Fei's hands toward him, palms facing up, holding his wrists in a punishing grip.

"Let go of me!"

"Quiet! Hold this."

Still forcing Shen-Fei into submission, he emptied whatever was wrapped in the cloth into his son's open palms.

It looked like a jagged stone, black with silvery lines running through it — a rather pretty but not especially remarkable dark lump, hardly bigger than a large egg. For the space of several breaths, nothing happened.

Then Shen-Fei began to shriek. His legs buckled and his arms shook uncontrollably, and the cry rang shrilly out, hoarse and unbroken. Slowly, black lines began to appear at his wrists. They pulsed and bubbled, creeping upward like distorted veins. Shen-Fei's eyes were wide and streaming as he tossed his head from side to side, clearly in agony, his piercing scream continuing, on and on.

Finally, long after his body had collapsed from under him and his knees had hit the floor, only the general's strength still holding the rest of him upright, Shen-Ya released his son's wrists. Shen-Fei fell forward on his side, still twitching uncontrollably, his arms held out in front of him as if burned, his scream dying to a sob. The stone fell from his hands, tumbling to the floor beside him. The black lines it had created now reached his elbows, and he stared at them, his mouth opening and shutting, attempting to speak.

"Boy. Look at me. I said *look at me!*"

Shen-Fei stared up at his father, his eyes wide and panicked. He gave a whimper, not unlike that of a wounded animal.

"Now you know what will happen if you disobey me. You will *not* send a message to the master healer. You will not so much as approach the palace until the proper mourning period has been observed. You will speak of this to no one. From now on, you will obey me in all things, as a dutiful son should. Now. Do. You. Understand?" Shen-Ya spoke each word deliberately, driving his point home.

Another wordless moan.

"Speak, or it will be all the worse for you."

"Y-yes . . ." Shen-Fei managed to choke out.

"Louder!"

"Yes, Father! I will obey . . . always . . ."

"Good." Shen-Ya's lip curled as he observed his son's distress. "Clean yourself up. You're in no fit state to be seen by anyone, least of all for the coming funeral rites." He turned on his heel and left the room.

Sai-Jun let the vision play out only a few moments longer, feeling the sweat beading on his forehead with the effort of maintaining the spell this long, then let his focus shift back outward. Slowly, the vision dissipated, the colors fading first, then the forms themselves, until finally, nothing at all was left. A moment later, the lamps in the chamber brightened once more, throwing the room back into stark relief.

Beside him, Shen-Fei's sleeve was held up to shield his face from view, his shoulders trembling, though he made no sound. Everyone else stood as still as stone.

"Lies!" The yell emerged, shattering the silence. Shen-Ya was visibly shaking. "This . . . this sorcery is a false vision. I would never—"

Lord Han-Zi stood. "Guards!" he called. "Arrest this man immediately!"

By his side, the guards jerked into action, approaching Shen-Ya, who continued to protest. "I am the general of Fo-shana! Do not dare touch me—I am your superior, you hear me? I command you, take not another step—"

"Did you kill Mother?" Shen-Fei's voice emerged in a whisper, and Sai-Jun gazed at him, his heart breaking at the sound. Never had he heard such a tone of despair. At this question, everyone stopped and stared at the young man, aghast. "*You killed her, didn't you? Why . . .*"

"*No!*" Taking advantage of the brief distraction, as the room erupted into chaos, Shen-Ya shouldered his way past the guards, who were unable to safely draw their swords with so many people in close proximity.

"Seize him!" Lord Han-Zi commanded.

Sai-Jun shoved Shen-Fei behind him, afraid Shen-Ya would attack his son in revenge now that all had been revealed, but the man ran past them. Before anyone could stop him, he burst through the doors, shoving them so hard that they crashed against the walls, and the guards ran after him, calling out a warning to their comrades in the hall outside, the cries echoing down the corridors.

"Stop him! Don't let him escape the palace . . ." The shouts and sounds of running faded into the distance.

Sai-Jun let out a breath and looked to Shen-Fei. "Are you all right . . ." he began, then stopped. Of course Shen-Fei was not. How could he be?

Shen-Fei stared up at him, offering something close to a smile, however broken. He gave a short, jerky nod, then let out a desperate sob and shook his head. He half-sat, half-fell to the floor, and the spiritual advisor pulled him close as Shen-Fei buried his keening cries—those he had never been given permission to release, even at his own mother's funeral rites — into Sai-Jun's chest.

CHAPTER TWELVE

Kneeling side by side with Sai-Jun, Shen-Fei bowed with him — Sai-Jun deeply and formally, Shen-Fei as deeply as he could before his bruised ribs stopped him, sending a jolt of pain down his side.

Lord Han-Zi bade them sit up. "We can dispense with the formalities, I think," he said, sighing and rubbing his temples.

After the pandemonium of the council had finally run its course, Lord Han-Zi had dismissed all from the meeting, asking to see both Sai-Jun and Shen-Fei privately once they had been given a chance to recompose themselves. The ruler of Foshana had changed into less formal robes, and they were alone but for the guards who stood outside both entrances to the small audience chamber, one pair by the main hall and another by the smaller garden doors.

"I believe we have all had enough of those for today," Lord Han-Zi continued. "Well. What a mess." He seemed to direct this last comment almost to himself.

"For which I deeply apologize, my lord." Sai-Jun glanced at Shen-Fei, as though to reassure himself he was all right after the recent events, then looked back at their ruler. "I can explain everything."

"No doubt. I certainly can't imagine you doing all this on a whim." Lord Han-Zi turned to Shen-Fei. "I thank you for coming," he said more gently. "I cannot imagine how difficult this all must have been for you."

"Thank you, my lord." Shen-Fei felt more or less recovered, though he was not looking forward to sleeping tonight, fearing he would be troubled by dark dreams. The hour was late, and putting off sleep to meet with Lord Han-Zi seemed almost a kindness—a welcome distraction from memories he wished he did not have. He bowed again. "If it were not for Sai-Jun, I would have never . . . my father would likely have gotten away with . . ."

He stopped. His father *had* gotten away with it, he reflected bitterly. His reputation destroyed in mere minutes and his guilt clear for all to see, he had nonetheless managed to flee the palace, and presumably the city. His life as an outcast might not be kind—perhaps he would roam the wilderness for years, avoiding most of society for fear of being identified and brought to justice—but he had avoided punishment all the same. Now Shen-Fei would never really know the truth of it. He had been able to tell his story—but what of his mother's?

Beside him, Sai-Jun, perhaps reading his tension, reached his arm out slightly, his wide sleeve obscuring the movement, and gave his hand a surreptitious squeeze.

Shen-Fei made himself focus on the present. For the moment, it was all he had. "Please don't punish Sai-Jun," he continued. "I know he must have broken certain rules to accomplish what he did. But if he hadn't convinced you to delay the council, or later stolen into my father's house, if he hadn't managed to locate the . . . whatever it was that did this to me, I don't know what would have happened."

"Punish him?" Lord Han-Zi seemed faintly astonished at the suggestion. "Quite the contrary. I have him to thank—like you, I cannot rightly say what would have occurred had your father remained in possession of such an object. I also cannot say what his plans were—if he had some ultimate goal he was trying to achieve—but such a dangerous item should not exist. It is simply too easily misused . . . as I have now seen with my own eyes." He looked at Sai-Jun. "Tomorrow it shall be destroyed. There will be witnesses—people you and I both personally trust—to make sure it is so."

"Of course, my lord."

"Good." Lord Han-Zi's voice turned more business-like. "Now, do we know how Shen-Ya came into possession of said item?"

"Unfortunately not, my lord. I can only assume he somehow came across it somewhere in the palace. We know from the vision that this occurred some years ago. Perhaps it was mere happenstance, or perhaps he located it intentionally. We may never know. Shen-Fei?"

Sai-Jun looked at him questioningly, and Shen-Fei shook his head. "I don't know either. I had no idea my father had such a thing until . . . well, it was as you saw." He cleared his throat uncomfortably. "If he had specific plans of any kind, he never divulged them to me. My lord, could it be . . . well, perhaps it had something to do with your own father? I don't mean to say he was directly involved," Shen-Fei added hastily, "but, well . . . torture was only outlawed in the final years of his reign. You say the item and all like it were to be destroyed, but by whom? If my father was given some responsibility for this, or if he was involved in any way, it's possible he simply stole it when the opportunity presented itself, whether he knew much about it or not."

"Hmm." Lord Han-Zi stroked his beard contemplatively. "My father regretted many things in his final years, the use of magical items for torture included. He rarely spoke of these things to me, but it is my belief he thought that, in times of such peace with which we are now blessed, it was a stain on the kingdom and an unhappy reminder of times past. I do not know, however, if he tasked Shen-Ya with the responsibility of doing anything in relation to this. Another mystery that will never be solved, I fear," he sighed.

"I'm sorry I cannot be of more help, my lord." Shen-Fei

gazed at the ground. "I . . . Shen-Ya was my father, after all. Perhaps there was something I could have done . . ." The thought struck him then—what if Lord Han-Zi felt that some of the guilt rested on Shen-Fei for allowing these events to happen? Would he, too, face some kind of punishment for having such a close relationship with the accused?

"Nonsense," Lord Han-Zi replied briskly, putting at least that particular fear to rest. "This is none of your doing." His attention turned back to Sai-Jun. "But I do have one more question for you, Sai-Jun. What we all witnessed tonight in the vision you conjured—how was such a thing possible?"

Sai-Jun looked briefly uncomfortable. "It was the second reason for my actions in stealing into Shen-Ya's home," he said. "At a time when I knew the general to be absent, and with Shen-Fei's knowledge, I made my way into each room, the household servants allowing me to do so despite their misgivings, as I bore a message directly from Shen-Fei. It was partially to search for the item, it is true, which I eventually located in Shen-Ya's own chambers. However, I also required . . . well, I suppose you'd call it energy, my lord, of a sort. When dramatic events happen, where incredibly strong emotions are released, particularly in enclosed spaces, this energy may often linger—occasionally even for years. When Shen-Fei told me what had happened to him, I sought to capture that energy. Think of it as a collection of . . . not memories, exactly, but impressions, that might be trapped in that space and coaxed to reawaken, given enough knowledge and spiritual abilities of the seeker. The result is what we all witnessed in the vision today."

"I see." Shen-Fei caught a look of pity in Lord Han-Zi's eyes as the ruler glanced briefly at him. "And no, ah, impressions of anything else? For example, what may have happened to the Lady Mei?"

Shen-Fei held his breath. He hadn't realized this was a

possibility.

"I'm afraid not," Sai-Jun replied, shaking his head, and Shen-Fei didn't know whether to feel disappointed or relieved. Part of him badly wanted to know beyond doubt the truth of the matter, but at the same time, he did not think he could have stood to watch if it turned out his father had indeed induced his mother's death, whether by poison or any other means. He squeezed his eyes briefly shut, not wanting to so much as imagine.

"Very well." Lord Han-Zi looked at them both. "Now, I have called you here not simply to establish the facts for myself, such as they can be ascertained, but to reward you. You have potentially averted tragedy and saved lives, for I think it likely that Shen-Ya had other plans in the far longer term than simply to possess a forbidden object. Perhaps even, eventually, some form of military coup. So. What can be done to repay your service?"

Shen-Fei gaped. He was not to be punished for what had occurred, but rewarded? He had not thought about this and had no answer to the question. Right now, he wanted nothing, except perhaps to be alone with Sai-Jun for comfort.

Next to him, Sai-Jun was also shaking his head. "I have no need of reward, my lord."

"And have the whole city gossiping that I neglected the hero who brought all this to light?" Lord Han-Zi huffed. "Not likely. The public may never know the full truth of the matter, but make no mistake, the fact that Shen-Ya was a traitor to his lord and to the laws of this province, and that Spiritual Advisor Sai-Jun, along with the general's own son, helped to vanquish him, will be all over the city by dawn. Enough people witnessed Shen-Ya flee the palace, and people will talk, even if I were to bid them be silent." He shrugged. "It is not within my power to stop idle gossip."

"Nonetheless." Sai-Jun bowed. "I respectfully refuse any

reward. Have that on public record if you must."

Lord Han-Zi clicked his tongue, seeing Shen-Fei's nod of agreement. "You, too, Shen-Fei? This will not do." He rested his chin in his hands, and Shen-Fei saw the calculating look in his eyes. "Nothing at all, you say?" he pressed.

Sai-Jun gave a scowl. "I know that look. What are you up to?"

"Hmph . . ." Lord Han-Zi's smile was more of a smirk. "I was merely thinking, what is to become of Shen-Fei now that his father is disappeared, likely never to return? Well? Any plans?"

This was directed at Shen-Fei, who shook his head, bewildered by the sudden shift in conversation, and the entirely casual way at which the lord of Foshana and the spiritual advisor were now seemingly conversing.

"No, my lord. I've barely been able to think of tomorrow, let alone further into the future. I suppose . . . I should return to my father's . . . I mean, return home. My father's servants still live there for the time being, though they are not large in number." The thought did not appeal to him. Though he might call it home, he had not been comfortable living in his father's house for many years. Even now that Shen-Ya was gone, did he want to take over the household and continue to live there, alone but for the few servants left to keep the place from ruin? Surely it was too large, and besides, he had never really given much thought to running a household. His father's presence had been far too dominant for that.

"What if you were to be invited to live here in the palace instead?" Lord Han-Zi asked him then. "If you were to be awarded your own apartments, if you were granted much the same rights as my faithful spiritual advisor here . . ."

Shen-Fei stared at him, mouth agape. Sai-Jun barely moved, apparently just as stunned, though his face, as usual, showed little. "I . . . my lord, that is . . ." It was all Shen-Fei could get out for a moment. He had no idea how to respond to such a question.

"I have it on good authority that you have quite the passion for the creation of artwork. If you feel as though your passion may lead you to your future path, perhaps an apprenticeship might be found . . ." Lord Han-Zi pressed.

"An apprenticeship . . ." The idea had never occurred to him, for despite his love of drawing, his father had always made it clear that Shen-Fei should never aspire to anything other than warriorhood, and if possible, to succeed him in the role of general, however unlikely that had seemed.

"It is true, you are not as young as most who are apprenticed," Lord Han-Zi continued, oblivious to Shen-Fei's astonishment. "Still, I would be remiss if I did not provide an opportunity for whatever natural skills you may possess to flourish. It is only your right, as it would be for any lawful citizen of Foshana."

"My lord. Perhaps we could discuss this later, in a few days' time, when we've . . . when Shen-Fei has had time to think on such a generous offer," Sai-Jun suggested when Shen-Fei still could not find the words to respond.

"Oh, very well," Lord Han-Zi grumbled. "Let me know when you've decided. But personally, I think you of all people would be a fool not to accept."

For some reason, Sai-Jun turned slightly red at this. "Yes, my lord." He leveled what appeared to be a warning look at the ruler, even glaring a little, and Shen-Fei stared. Surely Sai-Jun would be reprimanded for such open disrespect?

But Lord Han-Zi only grinned in response, a surprisingly boyish expression beneath his dark beard, and made a shooing motion. "Go on then, the pair of you. Have your . . . discussion. Take as long as you need."

Sai-Jun muttered something that sounded suspiciously like a curse and stood, gesturing for Shen-Fei to do the same. Then he straightened his shoulders, gathering up his formality about him again like a defensive cloak, though his face was still pink. He bowed. "Good night, my lord."

Lord Han-Zi nodded at them both as they made their farewells, the suggestion of a knowing smile on his face. "Rest well, the two of you. I dare say you've more than earned it."

CHAPTER THIRTEEN

The rest of the night slowly passed, Sai-Jun gladly sharing his bed with Shen-Fei and offering what comfort he could, though they were not intimate. It was clear that Shen-Fei had no wish to talk of what had happened that day, or of any time before. And so they spoke little, Sai-Jun simply holding the other close as they dozed on and off throughout the night. Several times, Shen-Fei awoke with a start, shuddering at whatever dreams pursued him, but even then, he made no sound, his heart pounding against Sai-Jun's chest, until his breathing eventually evened out again in sleep.

The next few days were busy ones for Sai-Jun, and he barely had time to talk even if he wanted to, for the ceremony of the changing seasons was upon them. He went about his duties as spiritual advisor with a vengeance, glad enough for the distraction.

Meanwhile, Shen-Fei was allowed to roam the palace as he wished, spending much of his time with only a stack of parchment and ink for company as he drew, though he had not yet been brave enough to show Sai-Jun the results of his work, and Sai-Jun did not press him to do so. Whenever Shen-Fei chose to leave the privacy of the spiritual advisor's apartments, Sai-Jun knew he hated that people stared. It would be some time before the young man would be known as anything other than the son of Shen-Ya, the disgraced ex-general who was wanted for his crimes and now living somewhere unknown as an outlaw of the province. When Sai-Jun remarked tartly that he thought people had better things to do than gape and gossip, pointedly staring coldly back until such gossipmongers at least had the decency to move out of sight and engage in their idle chatter in a more private setting, Shen-Fei only shook his head.

"I can't really blame them," he said. "Besides, I have better things to do than listen to it. I still need to decide what to do. I truly have no idea . . ." He bit his lip, looking achingly vulnerable.

"There's need to rush such a decision," Sai-Jun told him. "Don't let Lord Han-Zi push you into anything. Take your time, make up your own mind."

Shen-Fei nodded. "I need to go home, at least for a while. Even if the household is to be emptied and sold, it's my responsibility now to attend to such matters. There is nobody else left."

"If you need any help . . ."

Shen-Fei nodded. "I know. But I'll do what I can on my own for now. You're busy enough as it is, I know that."

"I can find the time," Sai-Jun assured him. "If not now, then in a few days . . ."

Shen-Fei only nodded, and for a while, this was as far as any talk of the future went. Sai-Jun had no wish to press him — Shen-Fei had more than enough on his mind as it was, and whenever he was to come to a decision about more long-term matters, the spiritual advisor wanted that choice to be Shen-Fei's alone. Sai-Jun had made it clear enough what he wanted — it was time to be patient and allow Shen-Fei to take charge of his own life, now that it was truly his for the first time.

So did the next several days progress, and when the rains began, there was still no word of Shen-Fei's father — not that Sai-Jun really expected any — and Shen-Fei still appeared restless, unable to make up his mind about what the future should hold for him. But when night fell, they continued to hold one another, listening to the rain and wondering silently, together in the darkness, about what was to come.

Sai-Jun watched Shen-Fei stir, muttering something in half-wakefulness. Unconsciously stretching, his eyes fluttered open, now registering the fact that Sai-Jun was staring at him, his face almost expressionless.

"Did you have another nightmare?"

Shen-Fei shook his head. "No . . . just a dream."

"What did you dream of?"

He felt the movement of Shen-Fei's shoulders as he shrugged. "I don't remember. I don't think it was anything bad . . . I was looking for someone, I think. When did you come to bed?"

Sai-Jun had been up late the night before, unable to quiet his mind enough to sleep and choosing to read through some historical scrolls, though he could barely remember a word of them. "Two or three hours after you, perhaps. You did not stir when I joined you."

Shen-Fei appeared deep in thought, turned toward the window at the gradually lightening sky. His breathing was easy, however, and his body relaxed.

"Shen-Fei?"

"Yes?"

"Are you all right?"

The young man nodded. "I'm fine. I guess to me, it just . . . doesn't really matter anymore. I asked you once not to have my father killed, but now, he might as well be dead. I doubt I'll ever see him again, and I've decided I don't want to. If he is ever brought to justice for his actions, let it be so out of my sight." Then, changing the subject abruptly, he turned to Sai-Jun, a strange mix of embarrassment and determination in his gaze. "I've been thinking about other things too. About what to do. About us . . ."

Sai-Jun strove to keep his expression neutral. "Ah," was all he could say.

To his surprise, Shen-Fei burst out laughing at that. "You're hiding your nerves, I can tell."

Sai-Jun relaxed a little at the sound. "Am I so easy to read?"

"No. Not to most people anyway. At least, I hope not. I like being the only one."

Sai-Jun felt relief knowing the layer of dimness in the pre-dawn light hid his embarrassment at this. "So happy you feel that way," he muttered.

Shen-Fei chuckled again, then sobered a little, though the hint of a smile still played about his mouth. "I've spoken to the servants in my father's . . . in my household. They are not many. Two, who were once my mother's servants, wish to return to their homes and seek employment there. The others requested to remain in the capital. I have no need of personal servants, but do you think, if positions might be found for them here in the palace—"

"Yes," said Sai-Jun, too quickly, and Shen-Fei grinned. "Then, does this mean . . ." He couldn't bring himself to ask outright in case he was wrong.

"Yes," Shen-Fei replied.

"Yes?" The spiritual advisor could barely believe his ears.

"Send a message to Lord Han-Zi, informing him that if it's still open to me, I accept his highly generous offer of—"

"Consider it done," Sai-Jun blurted. He felt almost giddy with relief.

"Good. I'm sorry it took me so long to say anything. I didn't mean to make you—"

Sai-Jun stopped his words with a kiss—the very first they'd shared, he realized, since that fateful night almost exactly a year ago. Not even during the time they had bathed together had they quite become so close as to re-share this act of emotional intimacy.

The kiss was gentle at first, even chaste. Then, like the rain that had started softly but now drummed hard against the palace walls, the kiss became something more forceful, and then frenzied.

The floodgates opened, and just like that, Sai-Jun barely knowing how it happened, they were pushing, pulling, stroking, loving . . . their bedclothes were tossed haphazardly about as they both hastened to get each other naked and into one another's arms in a flurry of arms and legs, the sheets tangling about them, straining to get closer, *closer*, neither attempting to disguise their sudden need or maintain even a semblance of dignity.

"Hurry . . ." It was a heated whisper against Sai-Jun's ear against a backdrop of squirming naked limbs, the slick sound of oil sliding over immodestly bare flesh when Sai-Jun, dazed, somehow remembered to retrieve the small vial of it he kept tucked away in a low cabinet beside the bed for just such a purpose. As he had touched himself in the days, weeks, months after their very first sexual encounter in the library a year ago, so he now touched Shen-Fei — excitedly, eagerly, not wanting to hurt, but afraid that if he did not have him now, his body might fly apart with the force of his want.

Shen-Fei gasped and then groaned as Sai-Jun pushed inside of him, the oil allowing smooth passage, the sound wet and explicit.

It only made Sai-Jun want him all the more, but he forced himself to hold back still. "Should I wait — "

"No! I want this, you've no idea — "

"Believe me, I do too."

"*Gods* — "

They did not last long. It was embarrassing, really — or it would have been, if either of them had the wherewithal to care. When Sai-Jun spilled himself, buried deep inside Shen-

Fei, an urgent and frantic release, Shen-Fei made a keening sound and found his own release only a moment later, his head thrown back as he shuddered in Sai-Jun's grasp, making no move to hide himself or push the other man away. This time, there was no physical self-consciousness, no need for pretense. This time, their need, no matter how raw, was perfect and whole in its honesty.

"Sai-Jun?"

"Yes?" There they still lay, panting unashamedly in each other's arms, the sweat slowly cooling on their skin, but both of them too hot to have the decency to yet cover themselves.

"I don't suppose, even with my own apartments in the palace, that people would care if we continued to share a bed?"

"I don't suppose so," Sai-Jun agreed lazily. For once, he didn't give a damn if people talked. Let them.

"I know it's hardly proper—"

"A bit too late to worry over such things now," Sai-Jun said. Though he knew he probably appeared foolish, he couldn't seem to stop smiling.

"Still. Don't you have a reputation to uphold?"

"Of course. And I will, have no doubt." With a wicked grin, he placed a hand on one of Shen-Fei's thighs, martialing his focus.

Shen-Fei jumped. "Oooh . . ." he gasped. His startled look gave way to one of appreciation. "I didn't know you could do *that.*"

"And much more," Sai-Jun assured him.

"Let a man breathe first!" Shen-Fei replied, though his eyes were sparkling.

"Hm. We'll see. Have you not heard? I'm not one to shirk my duties."

"I hope that's not all I am to you. A duty?"

Shen-Fei spoke the words only half-jokingly, and Sai-Jun did not hesitate. "No." He allowed his sincerity to show through. "Much more than that."

"Prove it, then. Again. Please?" Shen-Fei lay back, his head tilted and arms splayed to reveal his long neck and muscled chest.

Even Sai-Jun did not have the self-control in him it would have taken to refuse such a blatant invitation. He wasted no more time in thought.

Shen-Fei closed his eyes, another moan escaping him as, in accompaniment to their lovemaking, the rain outside continued to pour.

About the Author

Diana is an M/M romance author from New Zealand currently residing in New York. She has also previously lived in Japan and Thailand. She has no idea where in the world she'll be this time next year and is pretty okay with that.

www.ingramcontent.com/pod-product-compliance
Lightning Source LLC
Chambersburg PA
CBHW070503130626
46555CB00003B/1133